OFFSIDE WITH #55

PIPER RAYNE

This book is a work of fiction. Names, characters, places and incidents either are products of the author's imagination or are used fictitiously. Any resemblance to actual events or locales or persons, living or dead, is entirely coincidental.

© 2022 by Piper Rayne

Cover Design: Okay Creations

1st Line Editor: Joy Editing

2nd Line Editor: My Brother's Editor

Proofreader: My Brother's Editor

About Offside with #55

The last thing any professional hockey player wants is to be the old man in the game. The guy who doesn't know when it's time to retire. Still, I can't bear the thought of leaving the game.

This past year I've reflected on all my regrets, and I told myself that once I retire it'll be the time to find the right woman. But this is where it gets tricky.

I think I've found her—although she'll deny our connection to anyone who asks. We've been sleeping together casually and since I'm still playing hockey, I've let her get what she wants—me—whenever she wants.

After being told my career as a player is over, the owner of Florida Fury grants me a shot to stay in the game. A coaching position I didn't know I wanted until it was offered. The catch? He's also passing the family business down to his daughter.

Who's his daughter?

The woman who's been in and out of my bed for the past year. Which means the woman I intend to make mine is now my new boss.

Offside
with
#55

CHAPTER 1

"Take a look at the future of Florida Fury."

Kane

*T*he worst party you can attend as the guest of honor is a retirement party.

Who wants to be reminded that their glory days are over? Sure as hell not me.

When I retire, I don't want a party to celebrate my career—a career that's fucking over. Why would I want the reminder that I'm going to spend the latter half of my life not being a part of the thing I love? Hell to the fucking no.

I catch Coach Vittner's smile from across the room. Yeah, he's the kind of guy who enjoys a retirement party. His career has been long, always a coach, never a player. He treated us with respect, which isn't always the case in this industry. He embodies the ideal that as a coach, you don't have to be a screamer; you have to earn the respect of your players and then guide them.

This past year or so, that's exactly what I've tried to do for the younger Florida Fury players. Coach Vittner didn't have to tell me when I got traded to his team that it would most likely be my last. I had hoped to play for him until it was over though. Which leaves me at a crossroads.

We listen to Mr. Gerhardt, the team's owner, speak about Coach Vittner. It's a warmer and more thoughtful speech than a man like Mr. Gerhardt normally gives. He isn't exactly the touchy-feely type of guy.

After he's done, Mr. Gerhardt bends down and kisses his wife on the cheek, then his daughter, Jana. She looks so damn hot tonight, so I distract myself by looking at my plate, continuing to eat my meal until a big hand lands on my shoulder. I look up to see Mr. Gerhardt standing there.

"Excuse me, Kane, can I have a word?"

As if I'd tell the man no.

"Sure." I slide out from the table, ignoring my teammates' stares, and follow him to the side bar set up for the party.

He orders us two scotches. Scotch isn't really my thing, but I'm not an idiot.

"So, I was thinking about a few things," he starts. "As you know, we don't have a replacement for Vittner yet."

I nod. There have been rumors from the analysts for weeks. Some say Gerhardt's been flying places to talk with various people, and others say that longtime head coaches from other franchises have approached him. It's no secret that Fury has the talent to make a Cup run this year. Two skilled centers, a right wing and left wing who somehow know what the other is thinking. We play like a team that's been together for years, when in reality, last season was our first full year together.

"As you know, we drafted Matt McIntosh."

I sip my scotch because Matty is a damn good goalie. I mean, he's not me, but he's got the potential to be one of the best. The problem for me is that he's only twenty-two. A guy in his midthirties with the knees of an eighty-year-old can't keep up. I've given my all to my career and have the sore body and aching joints to show for it.

If Mr. Gerhardt is about to tell me that I'm out for Matty,

I'm going to stomp over to that microphone and announce my retirement because there's no way in hell I'll be one of those guys who doesn't know when his time is up. The guy who sticks around for yearly contracts, spending most of his time on the bench. Believe me, they all have their reasons. Some spend their money like hockey is a never-ending payday, so they have no choice but to stick around as long as possible to support their families, and others... well, others are like me. They don't want to leave the game. They don't want to skate off the ice into the spectator seats because there's an invisible line of no return.

"Yes, sir," I say to Mr. Gerhardt. "Matty's a great player."

"He is and he's got great potential, but he needs a veteran to teach him, guide him. I've been in this business a long time, and players like Matty either sink or swim. Either they can hold it together or they crumble under the pressure."

"Well, they're used to being the best in their league, then they come here and they're just *one* of the best. Hard pill to swallow." I remember my rookie year and shake my head at how cocky I was in that locker room. Ignorance really is bliss, I suppose.

"Listen." He puts his meaty hand on my shoulder and stares directly into my eyes. "I respect you too much to not be straight with you. Your career is in its sunset years. You might be able to squeeze this year out, but one injury and..."

I nod, not wanting to think about an injury that could take me out. I'm skating off that ice my last game no matter what.

"I need a coach, and Vittner says he thinks you're the guy."

All the air is sucked from my lungs and my eyes widen, my grip on the glass firmer.

As if he heard his name, Coach Vittner joins us, giving me a minute to recover.

Mr. Gerhardt orders another scotch.

"I've seen you with the boys this year. Especially Cory Freeman. No one can deny you're a natural leader, Burrows," Coach says.

I literally want to burst into tears because the door to my hockey career as a player is obviously swinging closed right now.

"You've had a great career. A few Cups, a lot of division titles, and a few records," Mr. Gerhardt says. "If I thought you had one more great year in you, I'd keep you on, but I don't. So, this is your opportunity to snatch up a great coaching position and hopefully win the Cup your first year."

My throat closes with the thought of trading my jersey for a suit. My stick for a clipboard. My skates for real shoes. But I'm not stupid or naive. They're putting the writing on the wall. Maybe I could find a contract with another team, but I'm way too scared to be a benched player, so I accept the offer.

"I'd love to. Thank you for the opportunity," I say.

Just like that, my hockey career as a player is over.

Done.

Finished.

Gerhardt looks at Vittner in shock. "Really? You don't want to think about it?"

I shake my head and plaster on a smile even though my stomach is revolting, and I feel as if I might throw up on Gerhardt's expensive shoes. "It's time. I'd rather stay in the game as a coach than watch from the other side of the glass."

Gerhardt smiles and puts out his hand. "That was a lot easier than I thought. Welcome aboard the coaching staff."

I shake his hand. "Thank you."

Vittner shakes my hand. "Smart man." He clasps his free hand over both ours and nods to me one last time before walking away.

"I'll get in touch with your agent ASAP, and we can figure out a contract that works for both of us. I wanted to see if you have any interest first."

I nod numbly. I'm not worried about it. Mr. Gerhardt has a reputation of being fair to all his players and staff. Besides, he could offer me a tenth of what I make now and I'd still take the job for the purpose of remaining a part of the game.

"Great. Great. Now come, I don't want anyone to be suspicious. Let's keep this between me and you until it's official."

"Perfect," I say. I think I need to make peace with this massive change in my life before the news is shared with others.

I head back to my table, doing my best to school my features. Tweetie rocks back on the two legs of his chair, obviously looking to get the scoop. They think the conversation was about my retirement and have no idea I just took a job as their new boss.

<hr>

AFTER DINNER, couples dance. I'm heading to the bathroom when I get pulled into a dark room. The smooth hand running down my chest is one I know all too well. She's a welcome distraction from my mind that's spinning out of control.

"Hey, you," Jana says, her fingers cupping my balls, her palm rubbing my dick from the outside of my pants.

"Hey yourself." I turn and fuss with the door handle. "It's locked now."

"We only have a little bit of time." She rises on her tiptoes and locates me in the dark, one hand landing on my cheek to center me before her lips touch mine.

I'm not going to lie. I've had women in my life, but none of them did to me what she does. Maybe it's the way she's always a little tentative when she initiates things between us. It shows me a side of her I never knew existed, as if she's scared I might turn her down.

Once our lips meet, it's like a cosmic force takes over and we both lose control. That connection, our chemistry is what keeps me coming back for more. Truth is, I'm more of a relationship type of person, but Jana's not. She doesn't want any strings. At first it pissed me off, but she's become an addiction I can't hold back from.

My hand rises up the slit in her dress I've been eyeing all night. As always, her panties are already wet for me, so I slide them over and thrust a finger inside her, making her moan and fall into my chest. I take her weight and rest my back along the shelves as I try to ignore the smell of bleach and cleaning chemicals, concentrating instead on Jana's perfume.

Her hand continues to rub, and our kiss grows more frantic and uncontrolled.

"God, I want you so bad right now," I whisper against her lips.

"Take me," she says before biting my lip then soothing it with a stroke of her tongue. "Right here."

My dick is so hard, and the dress she's wearing gives me easy access. She's already working my button and my zipper.

I'm about to say fuck it, I'm game, but the door opens, and the bright light pours into the small room and blinds me.

I squint at the door to find Cory and Ande standing with their jaws dropped, blatantly staring at us.

"Holy shit!" Cory's eyes are wide.

"You said you locked it!" Jana shouts and smacks me on the chest.

"Shit, so you two are really..." Cory says.

"Excuse us." Ande reaches past him for the door handle. "Carry on." She shuts the door.

"Damn it," Jana says. A few seconds later, the light in the room turns on and she's standing by the door, her hand on the switch. She straightens her dress and finger-combs her hair. "How bad do I look?"

"Jana, it's impossible for you to look bad," I mumble, tucking my still-hard dick inside my pants and buttoning them up.

"Ugh, don't you dare compliment me right now."

She opens the door, peering out into the hall before she bolts out of the storage room and slams the door shut, almost slamming it into my nose. I've managed my entire hockey career not to get a broken nose, and somehow it wouldn't surprise me that she would be the one to break it.

I leave the storage closet a few minutes later and go back to my seat, picking up my drink and sliding into the chair.

Shortly after, Mr. Gerhardt heads up to the podium. He's already given his speech about Coach Vittner, so I'm not sure what he's doing, but I hope we don't have to sit here long and suffer through another speech. I need to get the hell out of here as soon as possible. Jana got me so revved up in such a short time, it's all I can do to stay in this chair and not drag her out of here to finish what we started.

"Hey, everyone, gather round. I have an announcement to make," Mr. Gerhardt says.

Announcement? He's not thinking of announcing my acceptance of the coaching position, is he? No way. Nothing's been signed yet, and he said himself he didn't want anyone to know yet.

The room quiets down and everyone makes the journey back to their seats.

"When I bought the Florida Fury, I had hoped it would be where it is today. We're popular with our fans, and we've managed to grow the popularity of the game in a southern state, and we've built a solid foundation for our team. Now we just need to win the Cup. We've had a lot of growth these past few years, so I'm excited to announce who will be replacing Coach Vittner behind the bench next year."

My stomach crashes and I choke back the bile racing up my throat.

"I think this person can build on what Coach Vittner put together and with any luck, take us all the way there. I probably shouldn't even be saying this since nothing has been signed, but we've shaken hands on it, and I trust that we're both gentlemen and maybe I've spent a little too much time leaning on the bar tonight." He winks. "We're all like family here, so that means everyone has to keep their mouths shut until we're ready to announce it to the press. Agreed?"

A murmur of agreement goes through the crowd.

"He was a player himself, and although this will be his first year of coaching..."

Cory's head whips in my direction, but I continue to look straight ahead at Mr. Gerhardt. I knew he'd be the first one to figure it out.

"Kane Burrows has happily accepted the position. He'll be announcing his retirement from the league and taking over as head coach for the Florida Fury. Please welcome him in his new role to the organization."

The applause starts hesitantly, but it picks up as I stand and walk on numb feet to the podium and shake Mr. Gerhardt's hand. I raise my hand but say nothing.

He turns back toward the microphone. "There's one more announcement I'd like to make. I'm tired and I'm old, guys."

A few people laugh.

"So, I'm really happy my gorgeous wife gave birth to such an amazing daughter who's as smart as a whip and can probably take this team to places I could never imagine. Sometimes the old need to step out of the way for the young. Jana, come join me up here."

Jana looks at me like a doe in headlights, but her mom hugs her as if she won an Academy Award. When Jana reaches the podium, I slide out of her way as though it would be weird if we brushed up against each other, even though we were seconds away from fucking in the closet thirty minutes ago.

"It's yours now, sweetheart. The Florida Fury is yours. Time for you to take the keys to the castle so to speak. You belong in the owner's office." Mr. Gerhardt pushes his hand into his pocket and pulls out a key.

Jana accepts the key but doesn't say anything as he kisses her cheek.

"Take a look at the future of the Florida Fury, everyone." Mr. Gerhardt puts his hand out toward the two of us, standing next to one another with forced smiles.

My life went from simple to complicated in the span of an hour.

CHAPTER 2

"Ladies first."
—Kane

Jana

I spend the night processing the team dinner.

Getting caught in the storage closet with Kane.

Kane being named the new coach of the team.

My dad handing the team over to me.

It's a lot to process, to say the least.

Sure, there have been rumors about me taking over from the minute I came on board after I graduated college, but I never thought my dad would entrust a team on the brink of winning the Cup to me. Nor did I ever consider that Kane might be named head coach. That's a lot of change for a team the league knows will be one of the ones to beat this year.

With my coffee in hand and dressed in my favorite black power suit and heels, I walk into the offices of the Florida Fury, saying a quick hello to our receptionist, Tracy. She looks me up and down and sighs with what I think might be envy. Tracy is one of those young, impressionable girls who isn't yet comfortable in her own skin. Although in this moment, I feel a little like Tracy, which is the polar opposite of my usual confidence.

I head right to my dad's corner office. "Hey, Barbara, is he available?"

His assistant looks at me over the rim of the reading glasses resting on the tip of her nose. She's probably wondering where she fits in with my dad's new plans. It's just another one of the million things to consider in my new role. It might be awkward if she works as my assistant—she's known me since I was six.

"You know he's always available for you." She goes back to looking at her screen and types away.

"Thanks, Barbara." I walk past her, taking one last big breath before opening his door.

My dad is on his phone with his back to me, leaning back in his chair and staring at the view of the Gulf, talking about some vacation he's about to go on. I clear my throat so he knows I'm here and he swivels around, signaling for me to sit on one of the couches in the corner.

When I take a seat on his leather couch, I think about how it's almost comical how different our offices are. My dad's is all old money and "chief of the company" vibe. Dark wood, black leather couches, bookshelves lined with awards instead of reading material. Even one of his two pen holders looks as if it's from the 1980s.

He finishes his conversation and hangs up. "And to what do I owe this morning visit?"

I stare at him for a beat until he smiles and joins me, sitting in the chair next to me. He pats my knee and leans back.

"Dad." Somehow, I think I was able to convey everything going on in my head in that one word because he laughs.

"You deserve it. You can do it. Your mother and I are going to travel."

I place my coffee on the table in front of us and stare at him. "Why not just stay on for a bit? Maybe offer some guidance for the first year?"

At first the only response I get is a contemplative sigh. Then he speaks. "Sometimes I look around and I'm shocked at what I've built."

I want to throw a tantrum, fall into the couch and wiggle my arms and legs in a fit of annoyance, because he's going to tell me the same story he always does. How he came from nothing and built everything we have.

"I came from nothing immigrant parents who barely spoke English. They never would've thought it was possible, what I've achieved, but they moved here for the American dream. Maybe they weren't able to make it come true for themselves, but I did. And I didn't have anybody to fall back on."

I nod, hoping to make the story I've heard every time I've worried I can't do something my entire life go faster.

"If I failed, there was no life preserver waiting for me. I was going to sink. The pressure of that kept me going. Kept me from accepting failure. Everyone needs that, otherwise it's too easy to give up when times are hard."

"But—"

He shakes his head. "There is no but here, sweetie, there's just do it. I believe in you. Your mother believes in you."

"This is our year, Dad, and trades are going to be important. So much is resting on my shoulders now, and I'm not sure I'm qualified."

He laughs again, a full belly laugh, and he shakes his head as though he can't believe me. I don't usually doubt myself, but this is a *huge* responsibility. "You've been watching me work this team since you were little. You know what to do. Just have to trust your gut." His phone rings and he presses the speaker button on the phone next to him. "Yes, Barbara?"

"The movers are here," she says, and I swear she sniffles.

"Send them in."

"Dad, we're not finished."

He rises from his chair. "We are. Now you're going to move in here."

I shake my head. "I'm fine where I am."

He tilts his head. "Sweetie, for people to respect you, where do you need to be?"

I nod because my dad's corner office is the largest one with the best view. It's prestigious and screams "I'm in charge." Although I'll have to redo the office, I know I need to move in here.

"Okay," I say. "So you're not even going to keep any space here?"

"No, I'm retiring and leaving the team to you." He directs the movers to pack up the awards on the bookshelves before turning back to me. "Do you want anything? Bookshelves, desk?"

"That's okay."

"I figured." He turns back to the movers. "Everything will go."

I sit and watch the movers start to take apart my dad's office and my gut twists.

"First line of business is the press conference."

"Press conference?" My forehead wrinkles.

"Burrows needs to announce his retirement." He grabs his suit jacket from the hanger behind the door.

"Were you even going to tell me you scheduled a press conference?" I stand from the couch.

"I know what kind of worker you are. I knew you'd be here." He winks at me. "Let's go."

I take my coffee with me. At this point, I might as well

just put it in an IV. I have a feeling there's an unlimited number of days with little rest ahead of me.

WE GET DOWN to our pressroom where the postgame interviews happen. The Fury logo is splashed across the background, and chairs are tucked under the long table with several microphones lined up. The press aren't in yet because the sound tech guys are double-checking that everything is all set to go.

I walk out of the room to go find Kane and stop, seeing him coming out of the locker room down the hall. He's distracted, fixing his tie, and I take the opportunity to watch him for a moment, studying those strong hands that have moved my body into positions I never thought possible but are now fumbling with the silky fabric.

"Fuck," he murmurs and stops, his head hanging down from his sunken shoulders.

I should disappear. He's obviously having a moment, and we don't do moments. Our relationship has one mutual goal and that's getting the other one off.

I swivel on my heel to discreetly go back into the pressroom until I hear his whispered words. "Get it together, Burrows."

I've never heard Kane's voice anything other than cocky, arrogant, or confident, but his pep talk to himself stops me, making me turn back around to face him. His tie is completely undone and hanging around his neck, and he's staring at the ceiling with his back to me now.

"Hey!" I say loudly enough so he hears me and isn't surprised.

He circles around and shoots me his classic smirk, masking any of what I overheard. "Hey, lady boss."

His hands slide into the pockets of his slacks. I've seen him in a suit before, and as always, it makes my mouth water. I have a lot of appreciation for the way his broad shoulders and narrow waist fill it out. He looks so sophisticated and handsome right now, versus how rugged and sexy he looks after a game. I won't even let my mind go to how he looks after we've had sex.

"Don't call me that."

"Why?"

I approach him and take both ends of the tie. "Because..."

He watches me begin to knot his tie. "I can do it."

"I know you can," I say, even though in this moment, I think he might need a little help. "It's a big day for you."

His hands land on mine to stop me, and when I look up, I'm lost for a moment in his dark eyes. "I'm ready. I don't need anyone to pity me."

I smile because sometimes we're so similar it's scary. "Why would I feel pity for a man who was blessed to spend over fifteen years in a career playing the game he loves? And then when it comes to an end, he gets offered a coaching job. And not just any coaching job—head coach for the team every analyst is betting will make it to the Cup finals. So, Kane Burrows, don't go thinking you'll get any sympathy from me."

One side of his lips tips up and we lock eyes. I'm as transparent as Saran wrap to him, and for some reason, in this moment, it doesn't scare me like it usually does. He knows my feelings underlying the pep talk.

"Now your choice of ties... that deserves some pity." I knot his tie with a pattern I wouldn't have ever picked out.

"If you need a personal shopper, just call me. You're going to have to up your game in the suit department now that you'll be wearing one behind the bench."

"You'd probably make me wear pink or pastel."

I shrug. "Probably, but I'd get you labeled as the best-dressed coach in the league." I push up the knot on the tie, straighten out his collar, and smooth my hand down the silk fabric, feeling his stomach muscles tense under my touch.

He opens his mouth—I'm sure to tell me that he'd never wear anything I picked out—but the pressroom door opens, and my dad's voice booms through the hallway, making me step back and drop my hands from Kane.

"You ready, Burrows?" Dad's dress shoes click as he makes his way over to us.

"Yes, sir," Kane mumbles, putting a finger between his collar and his neck and tugging.

"Good. They're calling in the press now." He turns to me. "Jana, you ready to give his intro?"

My head rears back. "Sorry?"

"You're the owner of this team now. You need to start the press conference."

I thought I was going to be a bystander, watching from the side.

"You'll sit next to Kane at the table as he gives his speech about retiring. Then you can announce that he's accepted the position of head coach, then the press can ask questions of either of you."

"But..." I'm at a loss for words. "Shouldn't you tell them about me taking over first? Surely you want to have your last press conference."

"I hate the press. They're always a pain in the ass. They've all been briefed about me stepping down and you rising to the challenge."

I hate that expression. Rising to the challenge. It makes it sound as if I'm not really capable but I'm going to claw my way up there somehow.

I glance at Kane. Now I'm the one almost hyperventilating and wishing I could be swallowed up by the ground.

"Come on." My dad walks in first.

All I hear is the click of the cameras and people calling his name.

"Ladies first." Kane motions with his hand for me to go in.

The door almost shuts behind my dad. I'm ready to hold it open, but Kane grabs my wrist before I make it through the door. I turn to him, and he looks paler than normal. "Thanks."

"For what?" I cock my head.

He huffs, and that amazing smile he doesn't show often shines. "We both know what for. Knock 'em dead in there."

I nod, inhale, and step through the doors, feeling slightly more confident than I did a moment ago. Until the lights flash in my direction and I realize that people are referring to me as Miss Gerhardt now, instead of Jana.

CHAPTER 3

Kane

I'm used to press conferences. I've been doing them for over fifteen years, though I've never felt as uneasy as I do right now. I've thought about this moment many times, but it feels surreal that it's actually here.

Jana walks up the couple of stairs and pulls out her chair to sit down. The gentleman in me wants to tuck it in for her, but this isn't the place and she'd probably hammer a fist to my balls if I undermined her in front of everyone. I sit down next to her and position one of the microphones in front of me. She clears her throat, and the press all sit down like trained kindergarten kids listening to their teacher.

"Good morning, everyone. As most of you know, I'm Jana Gerhardt and I'm the new owner of the Florida Fury."

There are no whispers, which means Mr. Gerhardt did inform them of that change already.

"But we aren't here to talk about myself, but rather Kane Burrows. Kane, do you want to address everyone?" She leans back in her chair and allows me to take center stage.

I straighten my tie and bend toward the microphone. "I'm not gonna sit up here and lie. I've never done that and I'm not about to begin now. Today might be the hardest day of my life." I swallow past the dryness of my throat.

I practiced a more formal speech all last night, but it doesn't seem fitting, especially after what Jana said outside.

"I've been honored and privileged to play a sport I love all my adult life. Not a lot of guys have that opportunity and rarely do guys get as many years in the league as I have. I've won Cups and earned awards I never dreamed of. Played for Team Canada in the Olympics three times. I can't feel sorry for myself that it's come to an end. It was a great ride, and I've enjoyed every minute of it. But today, I'm here to announce that I'm officially retiring and hanging up my skates." A painful lump forms in my throat and I blink a few times when I feel myself wanting to tear up.

A few of the press snap some photos, and others raise their hands for questions.

Jana interjects, leaning into the microphone in front of her. "The exciting news today is that Kane Burrows might be retiring as a player, but he's signed on with the Florida Fury to take the head coaching position."

The room erupts into a mix of clicking shutters and reporters calling out questions as though they didn't hear the rumors that someone leaked from Coach Vittner's retirement party.

Jana puts up her hand like the lady boss she is to stop them from throwing out question after question. "Before we get to questions, the Florida Fury franchise would like to thank Kane Burrows for the brief time he spent with us as a player. He was an incredible goalie the past year and a half, and we wouldn't be in the position we are without him." Hands go up, but she's quick to speak again. "*And...*"

All the hands fall back down.

"We're thrilled to have Kane joining us as head coach. He's had a great relationship with the team while he's been here, and we know many of our players look up to him as a veteran player now turned coach." She glances at me as if she's stalling and allowing me to gather myself after announcing my retirement. But Jana doesn't have a sympathetic bone in her body, so I must be wrong. "And now I'll open it up for questions." She points at the woman in the front row. "Layna."

She stands. "We're sorry to see you go. Does this mean Matt McIntosh is your replacement? He's a little green, no?"

Damn, I thought the questions would start on a lighter note. There are other goalies on the team, but I can't lie and say that Matt isn't a prospect for a starting position.

"Matt is a heck of a goalie. He's excelled in his position, which is why he was drafted. But honestly, I've only been on the job for about twenty-four hours, so no decisions on lineups have been made."

Everyone laughs and so does Jana next to me. It shouldn't feel like she's on my side right now when things between us have always been clear. We use each other for sex and nothing more. She's certainly not head cheerleader in my cheering section.

"Okay, next," Jana says. "Hugo."

Shit. She has to pick a former player turned sports reporter, doesn't she?

Hugo stands and grins at me. "Retirement is hard. Most players suffer through the first year and struggle to find their footing in the real world. Going directly to coaching, are you going to be able to separate yourself?"

"Meaning?" I arch an eyebrow.

"Decisionwise. Players have different ideas of what should happen on the ice than the coaches a lot of times. Sometimes the risky play isn't always the best, and let's be honest, hockey players are risky."

He smiles at me, and I shake my head. Hugo was a teammate of mine when I'd just started out, but he retired shortly after. He once yelled at me for stepping outside the box to help him defend.

"I think all my years playing are going to help me be a great coach. I might have been risky when I came out of the draft, but I've learned lessons along the way too."

Hugo nods. "I hope retirement is good to you."

I nod my thanks as he sits back down.

Jana glances to me as if she can decipher what I'm thinking. Turning back to the microphone, she points with her manicured nail at the next person. "Ahmed."

"I think I speak for us all when I say I would've liked to see you play one more year. Win the Cup one last time... as a player."

"I'm sorry to disappoint."

The room fills with fake laughter.

"My question is, what do you think your chances are of winning the Cup? The Fury has been on the brink before and always fallen short. Drake with his drought one year, Ford not passing last year. Could something this year keep a team with so much skill from winning?"

I clear my throat and sit up straight. "I don't have a crystal ball, but if I had to put money on us, I would. We have two incredible centers. Our wings are unstoppable on all lines. Every player on this team would rather have a Cup than feed their ego. I've played in the league a long time, as you know, and there's something magical about this group of guys. You feel the energy in the locker room and when they're playing together, and that usually leads to success. I hope we see the Cup at the end of the season."

"And I have a question for you, Miss Gerhardt," Ahmed says, turning toward her.

"Yes?"

"Being a new owner, are you up to making the hard decisions that will inevitably have to be made?"

Jana's back goes straight, and she slides to the edge of her chair. She's like a cat slowly inching forward, ready to snatch up her prey. "Meaning?"

Tread carefully, Ahmed.

"Sometimes when trade opportunities come along, it's hard to separate business from personal, hard to not see the family behind the player."

I shut my eyes for a moment because any idiot knows he just misstepped.

"Are you suggesting that because I'm a woman, I can't make a hard decision on what's best for the team? That my heart and my emotions will be too invested and cloud my judgment?"

The tone in her voice is one that's been directed at me many times and I want to chuckle at Ahmed's paling face. He's a newer reporter and I'm fairly sure he didn't mean to offend her, but he's really stepped in it.

He raises a hand. "No. Not at all. I only asked because you're seen out and about with the players and their significant others. You have friendships with them, no?"

He's right. And the way Jana slides back in the chair, she knows it too. "You are correct. Many of the players have become my friends. But as most players know, decisions about trades are made all the time. In the end, this is a business."

Ahmed nods and sits without another word.

"And Ahmed?" she says. He rises back to his feet. "You're new, but ask around—I'm not really known for my warm and fuzzy heart."

The room erupts into laughter because, unfortunately, that is Jana's reputation. She's cold, calculated, and does what needs to be done. But I've seen glimpses of a different side of her, and I wish she'd let others see that as well.

We go around the room, and most of the questions revolve around my thoughts about specific players. Cory Freeman and Aiden Drake both being such dynamic centers, how will I choose who starts? Maksim needs help down in defense. Who might I have my eye on?

"Okay, last question, then we have to get back to work." Jana scans the room. "Tami."

I inwardly groan. Tami works for *All About Town*, a local magazine that comes out bimonthly and is always more interested in our personal lives than our performance on the ice. They just did a whole piece on Cory Freeman and his girl Ande's new place.

"Hi, Kane." Her flirtatious tone doesn't do anything for me, but I kind of like the way Jana glances at me to see my reaction.

Fat chance ever making her jealous. If I thought that would do the trick, I would've done it ages ago.

"Hey, Tami."

"Now that your playing days are over, will you be looking for that certain someone to fill the void?"

Jana licks her lips then sucks them into her mouth as though she's afraid she's going to laugh. She leans into the microphone. "Want me to tell you not to answer that question?"

The room laughs.

I shake my head and Jana slides back, crossing her arms.

"I'm not sure what void you mean. And not much has changed in my lifestyle except for the fact that I'm probably going to be busier than ever. I'll still be traveling like I did when I was a player, but instead of being able to relax after games, I'll be figuring out how we continue to win or how to fix what's not working if we lose. I'm not sure I'll have any more time than there ever was for a someone special."

Jana leans forward. "Thank—"

She's interrupted by Tami. "But why have you never settled down? You're not going to be young forever. You're already in your midthirties. Have you thought about going on *The Bachelor* or doing a dating auction for charity?"

"I'm sorry, Tami, but those are personal questions that Kane does not need to answer at a press conference about his retirement." Jana spears her with a look.

Tami stares at me, and I run my hands down my thighs but lean forward to answer.

"Jana is right, but I'll leave it at this. I'll date when I find the right woman. A woman who can handle my lifestyle. Not everyone can, no matter how much they say they can. And as far as *The Bachelor*, no. Charity auction, depends on the charity." I raise my hand. "Thank you everyone. Go Fury!"

I stand and leave the room, hearing Jana say her good-byes. Much to my amusement, she says "Go Fury" as well.

Once I'm outside the pressroom, I release all the tension in my shoulders and back. I'm officially retired as a player from professional hockey. It feels as if my career was only one play. It went by too fast.

"Thank god that's over," Jana says and walks by me in that power suit that shows off her amazing ass.

All I want to do is bury myself inside her and forget what just happened. But I'm not sure where we stand now that we're boss and employee. Time to figure it out. I pull out my cell phone and pull up the initials LB—short for Lady Boss.

Me: *My place? Twenty minutes.*

She rounds the corner, but I hear her heels stop. The three dots appear.

LB: *It's a workday.*

Me: *Play hooky with me?*

LB: *Tonight. My place. Seven.*

Me: *See you then.*

Three dots appear again, then nothing. So I pocket my phone and head to my new office.

CHAPTER 4

"Your wish, as always, Jana, is my command."
- Kane

Kane

$\mathcal{I}$'m getting ready to head over to Jana's when my phone rings where it sits on my dresser. I see my brother's name on the screen and press the speaker button.

"Hey," I answer.

"You seriously retired and never told Mom or me?"

"What does it matter?" I snatch my keys and grab my phone.

"This is huge, Kane. You didn't think the family should know? And you're going to be head coach now?"

My younger brother, Lee, knows how professional sports teams work, except instead of moving a stick around the ice, he's the quarterback for the San Francisco Kingsmen. My mom is always told how fortunate she is to have two professional athletes for sons. Not that she cares that much. She's stayed in her bubble ever since Dad died.

"Don't go acting like we're a normal family, Lee."

"I like to think we are."

I'm about to lock up my house when the guilt of his statement lands with a thud against my heart. "We are. It's just I'm used to—"

"Taking care of everything like a dad," Lee finishes for me. "I'm an adult now. With my own career. You don't have to take on that role. We can be siblings and friends now."

Lee is five years younger than me. Though it's not a massive age difference, it is when your mom falls into a depression and can barely function after her husband dies. Someone had to take responsibility for Lee, and that person was me.

I sigh and push a hand through my longer hair. "Okay. I retired."

He chuckles. I put the call through the Bluetooth in my truck after I climb in.

"Thanks," he says. "Glad I found out with the rest of the world."

Lee is good at guilt trips. It's how he got me to cancel plans in high school to go throw routes with him. How he convinced me to stay in with my girlfriend so we could all watch a movie together when I was a teenager. He was the worst when he wanted me to cook or bake something for him. But I guess that's what little brothers are for. These days, he's the one chasing me down, making sure our relationship doesn't disintegrate.

"Stop the pity party now. What's going on there? When are you playing in Florida next?" I pull out of my driveway, heading to Jana's expensive house that's probably paid for by her trust fund. Not like my little beach bungalow. But I like my house. I don't need much in my life.

"Next month we're headed to Miami. I checked your schedule and you're at home. Get that guest room ready. I'm staying at your place Monday and Tuesday, flying back early Wednesday."

"You don't wait for an invitation, do you?"

He laughs again. "I'll be dead before that ever happens."

He's not wrong, though it's not because I don't love him. I love my fucking brother to death.

"Do we invite Mom?" he asks.

The line falls silent for a moment. Both of us know the answer, but Lee is always more hopeful than I am.

"She won't come even if you invite her."

"True." Disappointment rings in his voice.

The guilt that got me to bake him my famous chocolate chip cookies back when we were younger rises like a tidal wave inside me. "Do you want to go out while you're here?"

"Nah," he answers. "How about we go fishing? Some brother bonding time?"

I can't deny that Lee makes me smile, the way he's always pushing our relationship. "I'll book the charter. Mind if some teammates come?"

"Not at all."

"Great." I pull down the road that leads to Jana's house. "All right, I gotta get going."

"Wait up a sec. That boss woman from the press conference? You two looked—"

I cut him off. "There's nothing there."

"Bullshit. I saw your body language. You forget I've known you my entire life. And when you're into a woman, your body language is a dead giveaway."

I park in the driveway of Jana's big house on the Gulf. She has more space than a single woman needs. "I have no idea what you're talking about."

"I've never sat that close to my team owner." He laughs. "Then again, he's not nearly as hot as yours."

"I'm hanging up now," I warn, and he laughs again.

"Kane and Jana kissing in a tree..."

"Bye, jackass." My thumb hovers over the screen of my phone while his laughter echoes through my truck.

"Love you, brother," he says.

"Love you."

We hang up, and I take a moment to sit and think.

Memories of our childhood flood my brain. Why do I still keep myself as an island when it comes to my family, even though my brother is always throwing me a life preserver to drag me back to them?

I should probably check in with Mom, but then again, she didn't call me. She probably has no idea I just retired.

Turning off all thoughts of my family, I set my intentions on Jana. Burying myself inside her. Feeling her soft curves pressed against my hard edges. Consuming myself in the physical pleasure we provide one another.

I climb out of my truck and walk up the pebbled walkway to her front door. The entire house is lit up like she's having a party. My finger presses the buzzer.

"Coming," she says from the other side of the door.

It's seven on the dot because Jana likes to keep on schedule. I used to fuck around with that schedule, coming a few minutes late just to piss her off, because going from screaming to fucking might be my biggest turn-on where she's concerned. It's probably why I can't stop being with Jana. The hate-to-lust thing is a real addiction where she's concerned.

She answers the door in the same black suit she had on earlier, except the jacket is off, leaving her in a silky light-purple tank that shows off the small muscles in her arms and her thin figure.

"Don't dress up for me or anything." She sips her wine and looks me up and down.

"You lock us up in the house." I'm not ashamed of my track pants and T-shirt with slides. If she allowed me to take her on a real date, it would be different, but she's only into booty calls—for the time being.

"You don't care to impress me?" She walks into her kitchen, and I follow.

Our homes couldn't be more different. Hers is white and bright. Not a lot of knickknacks, art that probably costs more than my entire house. Everything is modern. My house is mostly dark paint colors and rich woods. I'm not into the knickknack thing either, but I do have a crap ton of sports memorabilia.

I stop in her kitchen when I spot the white take-out cartons. "You ordered Chinese?"

"Do you not like Chinese food?" She sits down with a bottle of wine next to her and opens a container, pulling out a set of chopsticks.

I shake my head and look at her. "What's going on here?"

"What is your problem?" She digs her chopsticks into a dish and pulls out a bunch of noodles.

"We don't do food, we do sex." I cross my arms.

She finishes chewing. I wait, because as much as I'd be cool with changing up our relationship from fuck buddies to something more, Jana has always been the one with her foot on the brakes.

"That's what I wanted to talk to you about." She points at the set of chopsticks across the table from her. I sit in the seat next to her instead. She groans. "Seriously?"

"I've had a hell of a day. I don't want egg rolls and lo mein. I want you naked, coming around my cock and screaming my name." I lean back in the chair and raise an eyebrow at her.

"Those aren't on the menu tonight."

"I thought those were the only things on the menu. Is there a secret menu I don't know about?"

She giggles and continues to grab food with her chopsticks. "Our relationship has changed now."

I perk up, straightening in my chair. Has she finally come to her senses? I hate myself for the small seed of hope

I feel sprouting in my chest. "Good. Then let's ditch the Chinese food and I'll take you to dinner. I'll have to run home to—"

"No." She's quick to interrupt. "We're not moving forward, Kane. We're going backward."

Don't I feel like a schmuck. Seriously, how stupid was I not to figure this out sooner? That tiny seed in my chest withers and dies and falls like a boulder to the bottom of my stomach.

"The menu is now empty, I assume?" I manage to keep my voice even.

She places her chopsticks down and picks up her wine. "We don't have a choice. We're owner and coach now. A sexual relationship will only complicate things."

I stare at her for a beat, waiting for another excuse. She's been the owner's daughter the whole time I've been fucking her, and everyone knew Jana was going to take over some day. But I stop myself because I wasn't the coach. I was just a player.

"So what you're saying is that you can't control yourself around me?"

She giggles and sips her wine again. "I'm saying it's not ethical and if lines get blurred..."

"As in you realize I'm good for more than just orgasms?"

She gets that look on her face she always does when I make comments about only wanting me for the pleasure I give her. "Yes, which we both don't want."

"Says you. Don't go speaking for me."

That look in her eyes deepens. "I don't want a relationship. We've been over this."

Technically we haven't. I mean, yeah, she's made that much clear, but I never pressured her to tell me why. "Remind me again why that is?"

She brings one leg up to rest her foot on the edge of the chair. "I'm not meant to be in a relationship. Relationships are supposed to lead somewhere. I like my life plain and simple."

"Too bad you can't pleasure yourself, huh? Then you wouldn't need me or any other man at all."

"Stop it, Kane."

I hold my hands up, knowing if I push her too far, she'll close off completely. "Fine. So we're going to have a platonic, professional relationship from here on out, be cordial to one another?"

She shrugs. "It's the only way it can be."

"It's admirable that you can just shut it off like that." I pick up my own pair of chopsticks and dig into the chicken dish. As long as I'm here, I might as well eat.

"There's nothing to shut off. It was just sex. We can both find other partners to satisfy those needs."

The thought of Jana with another man makes me want to growl like a grizzly, but instead I chuckle and eat a piece of broccoli while looking at her.

She can fool herself, but I'm not gonna sit here and lie and say I could be as compatible with another woman as I am with her. From the first time we slept together, we just fit. I had high hopes that it might turn into something more, but she's hell-bent on maintaining her single status. I've tried to break down her wall, brick by brick, but she just puts them all back up. The woman is impossible. And now she has the excuse of the change in our professional relationship.

Then again, maybe she's right. Maybe I shouldn't be fucking the owner during my first year of coaching. Still, the idea leaves a sour taste in my mouth.

I lay my chopsticks on the napkin next to my plate and

slide out of my chair. "Your wish, as always, Jana, is my command. See you at the office." I wink and walk out of the kitchen.

"Kane, stop being so dramatic," she says to my back.

But I continue toward the door. The fact that she doesn't follow me tells me everything I need to know. No matter how hard I try, Jana might never break. I'm wasting my time.

The door shuts behind me, and I climb into my truck and drive away without putting up much of an argument, just like she wants me to.

Chapter 5

"Damn him and that whistle."

Jana

Paisley's been my best friend since childhood, but unfortunately, she's also dating the Fury's best defenseman, Maksim Petrov. She's the only one I've confided in about my relationship with Kane.

"Anything I say falls under patient-doctor privilege, right?" I sit in her office on the couch where a lot of the team's athletes come to talk to her about managing the pressures of competition.

"You mean the confidentiality clause? Well, you aren't paying me and we're best friends, but you know I don't tell anyone what we talk about." She hands me a cup of tea and sits in the chair next to me.

"Maksim?" I worry my bottom lip.

"Jana. I'm your best friend. You know you can trust me, so stop stalling and tell me what the hell is going on."

I called her in a panic this morning. After Kane left last night, I kept replaying the situation over and over in my head. Why he thought we'd continue on as normal when obviously our roles of owner and coach mean we have to end whatever it was we were doing. He's so presumptuous it's annoying.

"I ended it with Kane last night."

She sips her tea as if I said the sun is out today.

"Did you hear me?"

"Yeah."

"And?"

She sets her tea down and slips off her heels, then crosses her legs in the chair. "And I'm not surprised. I actually predicted it when the announcement came at Coach Vittner's retirement party about Kane becoming head coach. You forget how well I know you."

My forehead wrinkles for a moment. "Okay..."

"You guys have been sleeping together since Ford's wedding."

My head rears back. "No, we haven't."

She raises her eyebrows.

"Kane played the whole 'I want to date you' for months before he agreed to a casual hookup, so to say we've been sleeping together the whole time isn't accurate."

My best friend rolls her eyes.

After our first time sleeping together at Ford's destination wedding, Kane woke up the next morning assuming we'd enter into a relationship. Like he'd buy me flowers and we'd do lazy Sunday mornings with croissants and coffee kind of relationship. If he knew me at all, he'd know that isn't me.

"He bent to your will."

"I guess he couldn't resist." I laugh, and Paisley smiles but doesn't laugh. "Jesus, Pais, just spit it out already."

I love this woman as though she's my sister, but she's reserved and treads carefully. Hence the whole therapist profession. She tries to lead me to self-discovery, but sometimes a girl just needs someone to give it to her straight.

"I think if your dad hadn't changed this up, things would have progressed. Kane being named coach made for an easy reason for you to call things off."

"How do you figure?" I pick up my tea from the table.

"You guys were spending more time together. You said you spent that whole afternoon binge-watching that series about the con artist on Tinder."

I roll my eyes. "We also banged three times that day. I was really horny."

"Okay, but before that, it was like one would call the other late at night, usually Kane went to you, you had sex, then you kicked him out."

I lay my head on the back of the couch. "Ah, the good ol' days."

"Do you really feel that way?"

Here we go again with all her psychological bullshit. "Yes, I do. You know I'm not meant for a relationship, and Kane is definitely looking for one. Like I'm ever going to be at home waiting for him with an apron on and his favorite dinner on the table."

She opens her arms to gesture toward herself. "I'm with Maksim and I don't fill a 1950s housewife role."

"Come on. Look at Kane. I bet he wants a whole hockey team full of kids. Doesn't he seem like that? And me as a mother. Can you imagine? I'd be raising kids with ice blocks for hearts."

Paisley sighs. "I think that's a little dramatic."

"I'm not the 'let me kiss your boo and tell you it's fixed' kind of person. I'm the 'suck it up and get back out there' person. Youth sports? I'd be the nightmare parent on the sidelines."

She laughs and I quirk an eyebrow because she knows I'm right.

"Do you really know what Kane wants?"

"He wants a relationship, Pais."

She's quiet for a moment and I think I can almost claim

victory. "So you're planning on spending your entire life single?"

"What's wrong with that? I don't need a man to be happy."

Paisley puts up her one hand. "Of course you don't, but it sounds kind of lonely."

"That's only because you have Maksim and you're in love."

"Perhaps. Maybe I want my best friend to be as happy as I am."

I stare at her for a beat. "Happiness is different for everyone. What makes you happy might not make me happy."

She nods. "Fair enough. Why are you here if you're good with you and Kane not being sex friends?"

I shake my head. "Because now I have to work side by side with him, and you know he's not going to make that easy. He's always going to be saying sexual things to me and stuff."

"Then slam him with an HR write-up and sexual harassment charges," Paisley says as though it's so easy.

I shake my head. "I wouldn't do that."

"Because you like him." Her eyebrows rise.

"Oh cute, trying to catch me?" I bring my legs down from the couch and slip on my shoes. "I gotta get to work."

"So what's your plan?" Paisley asks, unfazed by how emotionally closed off I am.

"Simple. Ignore him. Do the bare minimum of what we need to work alongside one another."

"I doubt—"

"I run the team; he coaches. We shouldn't have to coexist that much."

Her head tilts. "But enough that you feel you had to call off your sexual relationship?"

I throw my hands in the air. "Jesus, Pais, aren't you on my side?" My hand moves to the doorknob.

"Always, which is why it's my responsibility to challenge you and not just accept your false beliefs because you're scared."

I turn sharply to face her. "I never said I was scared."

She smiles warmly at me. The way she does when she knows she has to say something I don't want to hear. "You don't have to."

"UGH!" I open the door and walk out, shutting the door a little harder than necessary.

Just because she's all in love doesn't mean I have to be. I'm perfectly happy going home to a clean house where I can watch what I want and eat nothing but popcorn for dinner.

I HEAD to my new office because at least there, things are simple. I have a to-do list, things that need to be checked off, and I can do them without any emotions or feelings or whatever this walnut-sized doubt in my stomach is. I don't owe Kane anything. My intentions were clear from day one. I never gave him any signals that there was a future with me. So, whatever. This guilt needs to stop.

After Dad moved all his belongings out, I arranged to have the dark wood painted white, and my designer, Kit, is hard at work making the space reflect me.

Barbara stops me as I approach. "The painters are in there. Kit was here about an hour ago and left you this message." She hands me a piece of paper. "Your father called and said they might be out of cell phone range for a day or two while they're on the cruise." Another piece of paper with a scribbled note is handed to me. "And Kane Burrows called up from downstairs, but he didn't leave you a message. He said you know where to find him." She hands me another piece of paper. "I wrote it down even though he said not to."

I smile. "Thank you, Barbara."

I wasn't too keen on having an assistant, but I'm not going to get rid of Barbara. I'm not sure how many more paper messages I can handle though. Just text me like everyone else in the free world.

"I'm going to head to my old office to get some things done."

She nods. "Don't forget about Mr. Burrows. He doesn't seem like a guy who likes to wait."

I inwardly roll my eyes and walk away from my dad's... er, my new office and toward my old office, but at the last second, I take a detour down the elevator. Through the concrete hallways, I follow Kane's authoritative voice to the ice.

The players are doing drills and he's yelling, blowing his whistle, and yelling more.

I smile, spotting Imogen in one of the seats higher up in the stands, and join her. "Hey you. What are you doing?"

She scribbles something on her notepad. "Trying to see who we should hype this season. It might be Kane, actually." She looks at me from the corner of her eye as if worried I might object.

Kane is now one of the youngest coaches in the league, and the fact he's head coach means even more. I can't overlook that.

"Plus, he's single, which you always like." She elbows me.

"But I've been proven wrong, first by your guy and then Cory."

Imogen is married to Warner Langley, our starting left wing, and just gave birth to their baby boy, Jalen.

"They are loving the pictures of Jalen." She smiles in a way I've only seen new mothers do when they think about their babies.

"Maybe because his mom dresses him in the cutest outfits and has made him an Instagram sensation."

We both laugh, but the whistle blowing startles me.

"Damn him and that whistle. Someone should take it away." I scowl at Kane even if he's not looking this way.

"The boys look exhausted. Warner said the practices are rough. I think Kane's trying to make sure they see him as coach and not teammate."

I lean back in my seat, observing. He is being hard on them, so I agree with Imogen—he's clearly making a point.

"Okay, that's it, guys. Shower up and don't forget to be at the airport on time for our flight to Oregon," Kane says to them all.

Warner looks up at Imogen and she blows him a kiss, a strangled cry leaking out of her once he's skated off the ice. I usually try not to pry—oh, who am I kidding? I always pry.

"What's up?" I rub her back for a second.

"It's the first time Warner will be away from us... from Jalen."

"Oh." I nod.

A tear trickles down her cheek. "We knew I couldn't go with them. Jalen needs to be set in his routine. It's just hard. And next week they're gone, like, three days. I'm being stupid." She wipes away another tear.

I wrap my arm around her, thankful the guys are filing out through the cave and to the locker room. "It's okay. I can help. Or I mean, maybe Lena's a better option. But I'll be there for moral support."

She laughs into my chest, most likely agreeing that I'm not the one to call when you need help with a baby. "It's okay. We'll be fine. It's just... you know... when you miss someone."

I think for a moment and get this weird feeling in my chest because at no time in my life have I missed someone like that. Other than my parents when they sent me to camps as a child, and maybe Paisley while she was in school. But I don't tell Imogen that. I just say "uh-huh" and continue running my hand down her back.

The sound of a throat clearing interrupts us, and we both look over at Kane.

"For heaven's sake, you married a hockey player. What did you expect?" Kane asks her.

I shoot him a glare. She's hormonal. Give the girl a break.

Imogen draws back from me. "I don't expect you to understand, Mr. I Sleep With Whoever And I Don't Want Any Strings." She stands and stomps away.

I watch her go, ignoring the fact that Kane is staring at me.

"She's gone," he says, and I tear my vision away from where she went and over to him.

"What do you want?"

"We need to talk." He sits down next to me.

I blow out a breath and roll my eyes, preparing to defend my decisions yet again.

CHAPTER 6

"Are you questioning me?"
—Kane

Jana

"**B**arbara is bothered by the fact that you won't leave messages for her to write down," I say as an attempt to detour away from where I know this conversation is going.

"Tell her I'm sorry." He leans forward with his arms on his knees and his hands clasped together. "Your dad always plans an annual trip for the guys. Right after the exhibition games, he'd plan a team outing before the season starts. The guys are asking."

Shit, I completely forgot about that. But then again, my dad was always there with them on whatever team-building event he chose, and I didn't have to be a part of it.

"He didn't have anything planned already?" That seems completely unlike my father. He never even gave me a heads-up to plan something in his absence. He really did just throw everything in my lap to figure out.

"My guess is no. Usually we've heard by now. Warner is especially wanting to know."

I hem and haw. "Can't blame the guy. He has a newborn at home."

"Imogen has plenty of help. He needs to suck it up."

Shocked, I study Kane. I've never heard that bite to his tone. He and Warner started on this team at the same time, and I thought they had a closer bond than he has with a lot of the other players.

"What? I'm not all teddy bear," he answers my questioning glare.

I know exactly how all not teddy bear Kane Burrows can be. The thought is a reminder of Kane in the bedroom, where nothing about him is as soft as a teddy bear. It's what makes us so compatible. He likes to be bossy, and I don't mind being a tad submissive if I get what I want in the end. It's kind of nice not having to make all the decisions all the time, and the bedroom is one place where Kane likes to be the one making the demands. My body heats from my memories of our time together. The screams, the pleas, the begging, the exhaustion. The man knows his way around a woman's body, that's for damn sure.

I look up at him and he smirks as though he can read my thoughts.

"What?" I scowl.

"Nothing. I just love seeing you blush."

I cover my cheeks with my hands and groan. They're warm.

"Back to team building," I say, wanting to escape this and go bury my head in work in my office.

"I'm not sure you'll find many options now. We could try to find a company..."

The thought of me going away on a trip and having to be around Kane twenty-four seven for days on end feels like a punishment. With my luck, we'd be on the same team, and I'd have to hold myself back from making a move the entire trip. He does this whole flirting thing that makes my body float toward his as though we're in the water and he has me attached to a string he keeps tugging closer.

"I think we'll just cancel it this year. Most of the team

hangs out together on a regular basis. We don't need to do anything special." I stand from my seat. "Anything else?"

His gaze rakes over my body, and it takes all my concentration not to squirm under his appraisal. "I'd ask you for dinner, but I already know the answer."

"Very well then. Have fun in Oregon. Make sure the guys stand out in these exhibition games."

Before I can beg him to bang me on the disgusting arena floor, I walk away through one of the tunnels to get back to my office. I forgot the power he wielded when I wasn't in his bed on a regular basis. The way my body begs for me to stop fighting him. I need to do one thing and that's stay away from Kane Burrows.

THE NEXT NIGHT, I'm sitting on my couch with a bowl of popcorn, watching the exhibition game against Oregon.

The announcers are obsessed with talking about Kane and our team because, as they put it, my father decided to take a team who had every element to win and set a bomb to it. Kane is too young to coach, I'm not equipped to run the team, blah, blah, blah.

By the third period, I shut off the commentary.

But that doesn't stop my brain from running their judgments and predictions through my head. Are they right? Maybe I can't run a professional hockey team.

Thankfully, my phone rings. I answer for the distraction alone.

"Hey, Dad."

"Why aren't you at the exhibition game?"

"Well, hello to you too. How is the cruise or whatever trip you're on?"

My mom snatches the phone away. "Sweetie, we're good. The ocean is amazing. You really should've come."

"She can't come. She's running the team," my dad says in the background. "Give me back the phone, Charlotte."

"I can talk to my daughter. I gave birth to her, you know."

Oh boy, here we go.

"Hours upon hours of waiting for her, taking her time to come out. Just because you like to think she's a mini you doesn't mean she's not part of me too."

"I'm going to the bar," my dad says farther in the background, and I hear the cabin door shut.

"Already tired of one another?" I ask wryly.

"He tries to tell everyone how to do their job. I mean, your father doesn't know the first thing about boats this big, but he tells the captain what he thinks he's doing wrong, and he complains about their liquor all the time."

I hate this part of my parents' relationship. Being an only child, I've had to play referee many times over the years. I know they love one another, but I knew this day would come. I had hoped it would take longer, but I'm sure eventually my dad will find a pet project and my mom will go back to enjoying her brunches with friends and her time alone.

"Just enjoy one another."

"Oh please, your father doesn't understand foreplay."

Oh, sweet Jesus. Can we please not go there? She once asked me where I buy my vibrators. Something a mother should never ask her daughter.

"Mom." I sigh.

"I know, I know. You don't want to hear about us in bed, but I can't talk to your aunt Ginny about it. According to her, Uncle Phil still goes down on her. Your father stopped that years ago."

"Mom!" I screech. Oh god, now I have visions of Ginny and Phil running through my head. Make it stop.

"I don't know how you do it. No sex ever."

I tilt my head, and thankfully, the game goes to commercial. "I'm sorry?"

"You never have a boyfriend. I get that toys can help and sure, sometimes I prefer them over your dad's quickies, a.k.a. let me get my rocks off and leave you unsatisfied, but you have to miss the real thing."

I pull the phone away from my ear, wishing my dad could stop this conversation from going any further. "I hate to alarm you, but just because I don't date doesn't mean I'm not having sex."

"You hire escorts?" Her voice rises about ten octaves.

"Uh... no."

"Then what?"

"Listen, I gotta watch the game. Continue having fun."

"Did you not hear me? There is no fun—"

"Just try, Mom. It will be an adjustment having Dad around more, but you can do it. You and Dad never get away. There has to be something you love about him since you've stayed married to him this long."

"His money. That's what I love about him." She laughs, but there have been times in my life that I believed that might be the only reason she stuck around.

"The bar is closed. What kind of boat is this?" My dad has obviously returned to the room. "Are you still talking to Jana?"

"We're hanging up right now."

"Let me just talk to her quick."

They wrestle like children and eventually my dad wins. The first thing I hear is his breath over the receiver.

"Are you watching the game? I can't get it anywhere. This place is like a black hole."

"We're down by one. Third period."

He blows out a breath. "I told Burrows we had to start strong. First exhibition I wanted a win."

I open my mouth but decide to say nothing. I thought I was the owner now.

"I mean, that's what you should be expecting. Are you having meetings with Burrows? You have to stay on top of him with the expectations for this team. He's new and I'm sure he has his way of doing things, but that doesn't mean they're right."

I listen to my dad. He's right to a certain extent, but instead of really grooming me for this position, I feel like my dad just tossed me into the water and expected me to swim as though it's instinctual or something.

"I'm sure he wants to win," I say, because who wouldn't? I doubt Kane would try to lose.

"He might think he wants to feel out the team. Change lines. Every coach has their own way of doing things, but the owner is responsible for keeping the coach's collar just snug enough that he knows he can't go rogue."

"Oh. Okay."

"That's all you have to say? Where is the pit bull I knew would get this job done?"

"She's right here, Dad. Go enjoy your vacation. I've got this handled."

"Text me afterward and tell me the score."

"Okay. Love you. Night." I hang up and drop my cell phone on the couch.

Now I have the analysts' and my dad's words running on repeat through my head.

I turn up the volume on the television. There aren't but two minutes left and we're still down one goal.

Kane switches out Aiden Drake, our starting center, for Cory Freeman. They're both great centers, but Drake has the experience Cory lacks.

"What are you doing?" I whisper.

Cory has the puck, and the time on the clock is slowly dwindling. Warner gets free, but Cory passes it to Ford, who at least has the common sense to pass it to Warner, who has the angle for the shot. But Oregon already knows what's happening because they have their veterans on the ice. Warner's shot gets blocked, and the puck goes flying into an Oregon team member's stick on the other side of the ice.

Cory chases it and Maksim tries to defend, but it all goes to shit in a matter of seconds when the puck gets by our rookie, Matt McIntosh, and the red light shines, making Oregon up by two.

There's one minute left on the clock. Kane calls time-out.

Why would he not have kept Drake in?

It goes to commercial, and I sit on the edge of my sofa, waiting for this to be over. My dad's words about winning this game and needing to show our competition that we're still the team to beat this year rings through in my head.

Finally, the commercial ends and the cameras show our players getting back on the ice.

Kane keeps Freeman in, and I clench my fists. Drake should be the man on the ice right now.

The puck is everywhere, our team doing their damndest to score a goal, let alone two, but we'd have to have four-leaf clovers up our asses for that to happen.

None of it comes to fruition and we lose by two goals.

The commentators dig right in that my dad made the wrong choice in Kane and questioning why I'm not there. My dad never really went to away games, so why would I? Screw the commentators. I'd give them a big middle finger if they were in front of me.

I pick up my cell phone and call Kane, but it goes directly to voice mail. Instead of answering my phone call, the owner of the team he coaches, he walks with the guys into the locker room.

Two minutes later, my phone rings and his name comes on the screen.

"Why the hell would you put Freeman in?"

"I'm sorry. Are you questioning me?" His tone is defensive, but I continue drilling.

"In a situation like that, Drake should be in. He's the veteran player. He knows how to play it safe. Freeman lost the puck, and we got another goal against us."

"Listen, Jana, I've got to do the press conference now and you need to cool down. We can discuss the moves I made and why I made them tomorrow when I'm back."

"Don't you hang up on me," I say. "Do you have any idea how important this season is? How much both of our reputations ride on it? You can't just go rogue and do what you want."

He laughs and I hear a door shut. "Careful, you sound a lot like your father. Of course I know how important this season is. I don't want to be the reason these guys don't win a Cup, but it's an exhibition game. It's for me to feel out the players, see where they fit. Drake played the majority of the game, and it was Freeman's turn. Oregon is good, our biggest competitors this season. Now I'm going to go talk to our team and you're going to calm down."

"Don't tell me what I'm going to do!" I shout.

"Bye, Jana."

"Don't hang up on me!"

The line dies and I stare at the phone in disbelief. What the hell?

CHAPTER 7

"What do you want from me?"
– Jana

Kane

*J*ana is fortunate I had to travel thousands of miles last night before coming face-to-face with her this morning. This dynamic between us won't work if she's going to call me after every game, questioning my every decision.

I take the elevator up to the team's offices. Although I'm technically management now, I keep myself downstairs by the locker room as much as I can. There's a clear distinction between the people up here and the rest of us down below and I'd like to keep it like that.

A few faces turn in my direction as I round the corner of the hallway, and I dodge the people leaving the break room with hot coffees in hand.

"Coach Burrows," a woman mumbles with a slight nod, sliding her back to the wall to let me through.

I wince since I'm still not used to the coach moniker before my last name.

I knock on the door that reads Jana Gerhardt, but no one answers, so I stomp down to the other end of the hallway where her new office is. Sure enough, she's there in the owner's office, talking to a woman I assume is a designer about what she likes and doesn't like.

Barbara slides her chair out to stand. "Sorry, Mr. Burrows, she's in a meeting."

I put my hand up for her to stay seated. "It will only take a minute."

"Mr. Burrows, she's not to be interrupted."

"Jana," I announce myself, standing in the doorway. "We need to have a word."

She glances my way. She knows exactly why I'm here. Did she really think I would just let that phone conversation after the game go?

"I'm busy, Kane. I'll come find you in an hour or so."

I want to press her, just to piss her off as much as I am right now, but I step back. "I'll wait."

So I take a seat along the wall across from Barbara. Barbara stares long and hard at me as though she's my teacher and I disobeyed her. Then she types again. What on earth is she always typing?

"How are you liking your new boss?" I ask Barbara after a few minutes of silence.

She glances at me then back at her screen. "I've always enjoyed Jana."

"That wasn't my question."

She leans back in her chair and huffs. "What do you want me to say? I clearly don't have the same relationship with her that you do."

My forehead wrinkles. "What is that supposed to mean?"

"It means I wouldn't bulldoze my way into her office without an appointment." Her eyebrows rise and a curl falls into her line of vision. She blows it out of the way as if it would take too much time for her to move it with her fingers.

The phone rings, which is for the best, because I'm so

angry I'm about to say something I'll regret. Then I consider the fact that here I am waiting on Jana—again.

"You know what?" I stand and walk over to Barbara's desk.

She scribbles a handwritten note on a pad of paper and holds up her index finger.

"She can come find me." I walk out and back through the maze of offices to the elevators, then go down to where I feel comfortable.

The guys are starting to show up for practice. They all greet me, and I mumble hellos, heading to my office. The small space is still pretty bare. All of Coach Vittner's plaques, awards, and pictures with players are gone, leaving the walls a beat-up, stark white. I haven't had the time, nor do I have the personal effects, to make this my space. The whiteboard in the corner is all I need for now.

I go over a new play I've been working on. We have our powerhouses on the wings. Ford and Warner are unstoppable, but they're becoming a little too predictable. Oregon proved that yesterday when they seemed to know what play we were going to run before we even did it.

A half hour later, the hairs on the back of my neck stand up, and I look up from my notes to find Jana in my doorway.

"What is your problem? Maybe I need to remind you how the hierarchy works around here." She steps in and shuts the door.

I lean back in my chair. This would be a helluva lot easier if I wasn't so fucking attracted to her. "Have a seat, Jana, but you can leave the attitude at the door. I've seen you come around my cock, my fingers, and my tongue. You're not going to intimidate me."

She remains standing. No surprise there. "You can't just

barge into my office. Whether you like it or not, there *is* a hierarchy here."

"You made it clear how that works last night."

"I stand by what I said." She crosses her arms. All it does is push up her breasts, something I do my best to ignore.

"And I'm going to say it again. You cannot tell me what to do on the ice. That's my job."

"I'm the owner."

"So you've played hockey? You want me to use a play you've been working on in our next game? How about you get out there and do some drills, show the guys some things."

She narrows her eyes, and they pierce into me.

Jesus, angry Jana gets me hot. It's childish, but when she gets like this, I want to see her bend to my will. I want to kiss her until she gives up the fight and lets me in, even if it's only her bed and not her heart.

"Funny, Kane."

"We all have roles here. Yours is not to worry about every little call made on the ice. That's my job and the players and the other coaches."

She's shaking her head before I even finish. "And guess who they blame when we don't win? Me." She points at herself.

"Hate to break it to you, but I'm right next to you for everyone's target practice if we don't win the Cup. We have the same goal. You don't have to bear the weight of all this by yourself. And you definitely don't have to call me to berate me for my decisions. I guarantee if my dick hadn't been inside you, you damn well wouldn't have talked to me the way you did last night."

She inhales and exhales slowly. "That's not true. I am your boss!" Her voice rises an octave.

"You make that abundantly clear, every fucking day."

Our eyes lock. She knows I mean it in more than just our owner and coach status, that she's the one who cut off our physical relationship too.

Her hands fly in the air. "What do you want from me?"

"I want you to stay in that new pretty office of yours. I want you out of my business as far as the calls I make during a game. You're the smartest woman I know, but you don't know shit about what's happening on that ice."

"But that's not me." Her voice lowers, and if I didn't know her, I'd say I heard a quiver.

"You need to force yourself or we'll never survive this season. You let me worry about what happens during the games and you can worry about everything else. It's the only way this is going to work."

She sighs. "I'm not sure I'm capable of that."

I come around my desk and sit on the edge in front of where she stands. "There's just a lot of personal shit between us. It's better if you stay in that ivory tower of yours and let me do the dirty work down here."

"That's how you see it, huh?"

"Let's not fool ourselves, princess. We've always been different people."

She nods, and for some reason, it feels like a slash to my chest. "Fine, but we better win this Cup."

"I promise." And although we lost the exhibition game, I know we can win the Cup. We have the best team in the league by far.

"Okay, Kane. You have it your way." She turns to head to the door.

"What? No apology?"

She scoffs. "Have a good day, Coach Burrows."

"You as well, Miss Gerhardt."

She walks out and screeches, "Jesus, put some clothes on."

I chuckle, hoping we've figured this out. I can't have Jana second-guessing my decisions all season.

Twenty minutes later, I'm on the ice with the team after their warm-ups.

Ford and Warner are having a competition on how many goals they can score against our new goalie.

"Come on, Matty boy, that was right there in the corner. Old man Kane would've had that." Ford laughs and skates across the ice, winking at me.

"Say it again and you're doing suicides," I tell him.

"It's all in good fun." He skates to a stop in front of me. "So, Jana was in your office earlier... we heard some yelling." He waggles his eyebrows.

Leave it to Ford to think we were banging. This is one of those moments where the line is blurred because I was their teammate only last year.

"You're on a thin line," I say.

"Lena loves it when we fight and then suddenly, we're all over each other."

"You don't have to share personal information." I glance at the playbook in my hands.

"What? I'm not being specific enough?" Ford teases. "Everyone knows the sex after you've been arguing is some of the best sex there is. Right, Drake?"

Drake shakes his head. "I don't kiss and tell. Let's get Langley's thoughts though, shall we?"

Everyone laughs.

"Fuck no. I don't wanna know about my sister," Ford says.

"No?" Warner has a shit-eating grin now. "How about the fact your sister's favorite position is..." Ford skates after him and Warner laughs, skating faster. "Come on, man, you've gotten soft again during the off-season."

"Screw you."

The two of them go at it for a few minutes before I blow my whistle and they stop in front of me, shoving one another like two siblings.

"Enough, guys." I give them both a look that says stop fucking around.

Everyone stands with their sticks in front of them and gives me their attention. They're all looking at me to lead them. To tell them how we get that win we missed out on last night. My heart rate picks up at their expectations. I meant what I said to Jana—I want the Cup. I don't want to disappoint these guys.

"It sucks we lost, and believe me, I've heard all the comments from the fucking analysts, but we didn't put our *A* game out there last night. We can all agree on that."

Most nod.

"We're the team to beat, and we need to show that out there every game, exhibition or not."

Maksim raises his hand.

"Yeah." I nod at him to speak.

"The team building?"

I shake my head. "It's a no."

"Thank fuck," Warner says.

"Tell my little sister she can get by for a few nights without you." Ford rolls his eyes.

Warner pushes Ford and he loses his footing for a second.

Other than Ford, there are some grumbles about us not having our annual team-building trip. Although I wasn't on the team that long, I know it's something Mr. Gerhardt has always done. Mostly because when I wasn't on the Fury and they'd show clips on ESPN, I'd be jealous as hell.

"Sorry, maybe later on, but with all these changes..." Then I realize I'm making excuses for Jana, and I wonder if she'd do the same for me. "Anyway, let's get to practicing. Ford and Warner, you're working with Tweetie and Train. Try to show them what you guys have on the ice."

They both raise their eyebrows.

"Coach, it's instinctual. I just know he's gonna be there," Warner says to me.

Ford nods. "Mostly it's me seeing him and knowing where he's going to pass. That's why I had more goals last year."

"You did not," Warner argues. "You had assists because I'm the better shooter."

"Just go." I wave them off. "Drake and Freeman, you're with me."

The practice begins, but I catch eyes on us halfway through. Jana stands high up in the arena and watches us with her arms crossed. I should've known she wouldn't listen. She doesn't listen to anyone. And damn if that isn't one of the things I like so much about her.

CHAPTER 8

Jana

For the past month, I've tried to keep away from the players' personal get-togethers. I just don't feel as though I fit now that I'm the owner of the team. But Paisley is my best friend and it's her party tonight. She and Maksim have a big announcement apparently, which means I have no choice but to go.

I ring the doorbell at their house and look over the cars in the driveway. They're all familiar, including Kane's truck.

"Jana!" Paisley opens the door and pulls me into her arms. "I'm so happy you came."

"Of course I'd come." I hug her then hand her the bottle of wine I brought.

"Thanks. You didn't have to go all out." She looks at the bottle. "But I guess now that you're getting paid an owner's salary..." She laughs, and I follow her into the house.

There are caterers in their kitchen and the majority of the party is outside, but the wives and girlfriends of the players I'm closest to are on the couch.

"Jana"—Saige stands and hugs me—"so good to see you. It's been a while."

I hug each one of them and look at Imogen, who's sans baby. "Where's Jalen?"

"Grandparents. Six weeks, baby." She grins.

I tilt my head, not understanding what she means.

"I can have sex again. Got the all clear this morning."

"I'm surprised you're here," Paisley says. "You didn't have to come."

"Oh yeah, I did. You can't tease me with a big announcement and expect me to hear about it secondhand. I had to drag Warner here with promises of lingerie and whipped cream."

They all laugh, and I smile, realizing I'm the odd one out in this group. The one without anyone special in her life. That ache hits me again, because one thing here isn't like the others and that thing is me.

Why can't I have a relationship? Even the small voice that tells me I don't want one second-guesses itself these days. I quickly brush it off as just being horny. Since I called it quits with Kane, I've yet to find anyone else.

Paisley brings me a glass of wine and I'm sipping it when I spot Kane outside with a hot brunette. They're laughing at something, and she puts her hand on his bicep as though he's a *Saturday Night Live* comedian. Kane has a lot of great attributes, but being funny isn't one of them.

"Jana?" Paisley questions, sitting on the couch next to me.

"I'm just going to head outside and say hi to the guys." I rise from the couch.

"Oh wait," Paisley says, but she just doesn't want me to make a scene. As I walk away, I hear her whisper, "Oh jeez."

"It's not what you think," Imogen calls after me, and I circle around.

"What are you guys talking about? I'm just going outside to see the guys and get some fresh air. Plus, I'm starving, and I see the table of food."

Lies. All lies, because I can't believe he brought a date. I guess I can't really fault him, but Kane has never brought a date to anything. Is this his way of trying to make me jealous to get me in his bed again? Not going to happen.

"Hey, guys," I say, waving when I step out onto the patio.

They're all sitting around the table with beers in hand. A few of them straighten up. The ones who don't know me very well.

Maksim stays slouched in his chair. "Jana," he says in his Russian accent. "Glad you came."

"Thanks for ditching game night last week," Ford says.

"Sorry, but I didn't have a partner."

"Kane came by himself." He raises his eyebrows.

Maksim rises from his chair to give it to me. "I have to go check on Paisley anyway."

I sit down and glance over my shoulder. Annabelle is with a few of the other kids from the team, playing in the grass just off the big patio. Now that she's two, you can see her and Ford's resemblance that much more. Those blue eyes are going to be heartbreakers.

"I saw that, Demetri!" Ford yells. "Jesus, Train, teach your damn kid to respect ladies."

Train shakes his head. "She took the watering can first," he sticks up for his son. He and his wife divorced a couple years back and share custody of their son.

I glance at Kane, growing angrier the more I see him smile and watch the woman touch him.

"Whatcha staring at?" Warner leans in and whispers.

I lean in too. "Nothing."

"I don't believe you. Maybe you should go introduce yourself."

I'm afraid if I do, my anger will get the best of me. Kane always seems to bring my anger to the surface. Then again, the longer I sit here, the madder I become. Like he's playing some game a high school boy would.

After zoning out for a bit, I rejoin the conversation. "Tell me how everyone's feeling about the season so far?"

Everyone puts a smile on their face, but no one actually says anything.

"The new uniforms?" I ask. Kane gave me an earful about those and how we didn't need them. But I wanted to go retro, and we can auction them off for charity as game-worn jerseys.

"Honestly, they're stiff," Ford says, the only truthful one here. Probably because if he loses his position, he has enough money for the entire team to live off of.

Speaking as someone with an equal amount of money, not much scares you because you know in the end, you'll be okay. But I appreciate his honesty.

"A few washes and they'll soften," I say.

But he gives me a half smile and carries on with Train about his kid taking another toy from Annabelle.

Damn Kane. He probably shared his view about the jerseys with the team. I can just imagine him being all, "Lady Boss wants us to wear these, I tried to give my opinion, but she won't listen."

For the past month, Kane and I have fought over every single thing from hotels to team dinners to the fucking water pressure in the showers. But I don't voice my opinion on what happens on the ice. My parents are still away and hopefully one hasn't killed the other because I haven't heard from either of them for a week. That's unusual, but I haven't been in the mood to seek them out.

I hear the woman's cackle again and I slide my chair out, my eyes on her and Kane. They stand on the far side of the patio, away from everyone else.

"Wait. Jana." Warner holds up his hand to stop me.

"Hey, hold up," Cory tries too.

Do they think I'm going to make a scene? I don't make scenes.

My heels click on the cement surrounding the pool that has a safety fence around it, which surprises me since Paisley and Maksim don't have kids.

Kane spots me first, glancing at me from the corner of his eye, and sips his beer, unbothered. The woman who has her back to me is clueless.

"Coach Burrows," I say, interjecting myself into their twosome. "I just wanted to come over and say hello."

"Miss Gerhardt, glad you could fit this get-together into your schedule. Seems you've been busy the past month, eh?"

The woman looks me up and down in the familiar way one does when they're sizing up the competition. A small part of me wants to tell her she *should* see me as her competition, and another wants to tell her I had him first. But I shake my head because aren't I the one who threw him back in the pond?

Sure I am, but he doesn't have to go throwing it in my face. My anger rises to the surface again. I could've brought a date tonight, but I didn't out of respect for Kane. Never mind the fact I don't have anyone right now.

"Yes, but Paisley's my best friend so..." I stick out my hand in the woman's direction. "I'm Jana Gerhardt, owner of the Florida Fury."

Her eyes bulge and a megawatt smile creases her lips. "Oh wow, I wanted to meet you."

"You did?" I tilt my head.

Kane snickers, and I shoot him a bored look.

"Of course. Kane told me about you, and I really wanted to thank you personally."

Is this woman serious? She wants to thank me because I'm not sleeping with the man anymore? And what exactly has Kane told her about me?

"What did Kane say?" I find myself asking.

"All great things. Just how you've been busy and didn't have much time—"

I block out the woman and turn to Kane. "Seriously?"

He sputters with his beer, barely able to swallow it. The guys at the table laugh, but I don't turn around to see what they're finding amusing. My gaze darts to Paisley inside the house. She looks ready to get up off the couch, her eyes on me.

"What?" Kane asks.

"You told her about me and why we're not sleeping together anymore? And then you bring her here for what? To make me jealous? I don't believe you."

He smirks and I want to slap it off his face. "Jana, this is Jennifer."

"I don't need to know her name. What's wrong with you? Our relationship was supposed to be private," I whisper, because he's the one who's outing us right now.

"Jana? Sweetie?" Paisley comes out onto the patio, shutting the door behind her.

I put up my hand to stop her. Paisley and I are different. She'd sit back and let this play out, but I'm not her, I'm calling Kane out on his shit whether it's right or wrong. Maybe I am making a scene, but only with this man who makes me crazy.

"Maksim! Get the stuff!" Paisley shouts.

"I didn't tell anyone anything," Kane says through clenched teeth.

"I should give you two a moment," Jennifer says, about to walk away.

"No. Don't worry about it, Jennifer. Let me fill you in on Kane's favorite kinks though, to give you a head start for tonight. He loves ropes and blindfolds—"

"Jana!" Paisley says. "Maksim!"

He rushes out from the side of the house with two canister-looking things in his hands.

"Shut up, Jana," Kane says. "You have no idea what you're talking about right now."

"One. Two. Three." Paisley does a countdown for some reason, but I ignore her.

"I don't, huh?" I put my hands on my hips. "Want me to tell her more specifics of what to expect tonight?"

"Go!" Paisley yells, and two big bursts of pink dust land on the three of us. "It's a girl!"

"Wait. What?" I turn to my best friend and see her and Maksim hugging.

"A girl," he coos, touching her stomach.

"You're pregnant?" I ask Paisley, who's looking at me over Maksim's shoulder.

She nods. "And that's Jennifer Mitchel. Her son had the Make-A-Wish to meet Aiden Drake."

"What did we miss?" Aiden walks back on the patio from the beach, hand in hand with a kid about five or six years old. "Sorry, Jennifer, he got a little wet."

Jennifer lowers to her haunches. "It's okay. Did you have fun, buddy?"

My mouth hangs open, and I want the earth to swallow me whole. "Ms. Mitchel, I'm—"

She picks up her son and rests him on her hip. "It's fine. Honestly."

"No. It isn't fine at all. What must you think of me? I swear…"

"Just let it go, Jana," Kane says in a soft voice, as though I'm the only one who can hear him bossing me around.

"It's okay, but you two should really talk this out." She directs her attention back to her son. "We've overstayed our visit anyway. Aiden, you've been so sweet to Ollie. I can't thank you enough." She steps over to talk some to Aiden while I stare at the ground.

"How did I not know we had Make-A-Wish set up?" I say the words to myself, but Kane answers.

"That's something you need to ask yourself." He shrugs.

There's absolutely no way I could've forgotten this. Clearly someone didn't inform me. I grab my phone out of my purse to check my schedule, and one of Barbara's handwritten notes floats to the cement.

Kane beats me to picking it up. "Look here."

He hands it over, and sure enough, it reads… *Make-A-Wish family coming this afternoon for Aiden Drake.*

My shoulders sink. I'm really starting to think maybe I'm not cut out for this job.

I shove my phone and the note in my purse, unable to even look at Kane. But Paisley is staring at me, so I walk over to her.

"I'm sorry. Congratulations! I can't believe you're pregnant. I'm going to be an aunt!" I hug her and squeeze a little tighter than I normally would. We're not related, but we've always said since we were young that if we ever had kids they'd call the other aunt.

She pulls away and smiles. "You're going to be the best aunt."

"So… baby before marriage, huh?" I smile.

She bites her lip.

"Pais?"

She cringes. "We had a minister come to the house and marry us as soon as we found out I was pregnant." She holds up her hand, showing off her wedding band. "I wanted to tell you so badly, but Maksim really wanted it to be a surprise and do this whole reveal thing today."

I realize in that moment how much things are changing and how out of touch I really am with all my friends.

CHAPTER 9

"It's the chick, I tell you."
—Obnoxious fan

Kane

Another month passes and our points have us as contenders, but I'll be honest, I had hoped we'd be better positioned at this point in the season. But it's still early days and we have plenty of time to make up ground.

The loss tonight was a tough one though, especially since Nashville is the worst team in the league.

I'm more than pissed off when I hear the razzing in the locker room after the game, so I walk out of my office to find Ford and Warner arguing about who fucked up the most plays tonight.

"What the fuck is going on out here?" I put my hands on my hips and stare at them.

They all freeze and look at me. I guess I can have that "pissed-off dad" tone sometimes.

"Nothing," Ford says.

"You guys think by deciding who was the worst player tonight, it's somehow gonna change the outcome? I'm not sure what the hell was going on out there tonight, but it wasn't professional hockey." I point in the direction of the rink.

Ford sits on the bench. "No."

"No, it's not. You guys have been playing half-assed all season. Do you think the Cup is just magically ours?

Because guess what? Oregon's beating down our damn doors and pretty soon everything..." I stop myself from repeating what all those analysts have said about Jana and me not being good enough to see this team through to the end. "We have to leave everything out there on the ice. Every game. I know you all have lives, wives, kids, and maybe you'd rather be home with them sometimes than here, but let me remind you, hockey is what gave you the life you enjoy. With the exception of Ford, you have the houses, the cars, the lifestyles because of hockey."

They all hang their heads. I've always tried to be an uplifting, inspiring coach, but not tonight. These guys need a reality check and a swift kick in the ass, and it's my job to give it to them.

"Now excuse me while I go attend another press conference where I give lame excuses for why we can't win against the worst team in the league." I swipe a water bottle off the shelf and storm out.

My night only gets shittier when I come face-to-face with Jana in the hallway.

I put up my hand. "Not now."

"We need to talk. How could we lose to Nashville? My dad's back from vacation. He was at the game tonight."

I stop before I open the door to the pressroom. Turning around to face her, I shove my hands in the pockets of my slacks. "So what? He's not my boss anymore."

"We both know that's not entirely true. He'll swipe this team out of my hands if he thinks I'm doing a shit job, which according to him, our record says I am. You have no idea how much lecturing I got up there."

I throw my hands in the air. "And what do you want me to do about it?"

"I want you to tell me what the hell is going on. We're

supposed to have the best team. How are we sitting where we are in points?"

"Let me get my crystal ball and see." I throw my hands in the air again. "I have no fucking clue."

"But we have the talent."

"Yes, we do."

"So is it the coaching?"

I jut out my jaw and stare at her. "Seriously?"

"I'm just saying we're the ones everyone should be chasing in points."

I shake my head. "I can't give you a specific reason we're not doing better. Let me have this press conference, calm down, and I can talk to you tomorrow." I twist the doorknob and start to open the door.

"I'm going with you." She steps up to the door and I let it close.

I sharply turn back and she's right there, her breasts pressed to my chest. After a night like the one I've had, the only thing I want is a beer and her. Preferably licking my beer off her naked skin.

"You're not going with me."

She scowls. "Why not?"

"Because those are vultures in there. Let me handle it."

She guffaws. "You think I can't handle myself?" She puts her hands on her hips in a "I am woman, hear me roar" gesture.

"I think you've kept yourself so far removed from the team these past couple of months that they're going to ask you questions you have no idea how to answer."

"*Ugh!*" She stomps a foot. I'm surprised her expensive stiletto doesn't snap. "You drive me absolutely crazy. I have not removed myself from this team."

"Fine." I twist the knob, opening the door, and gesture in front of me. "Have at it."

She smugly walks up to the table and chairs, positioning herself in front of the microphone. I sit next to her, and when our thighs touch, she's quick to scoot away. I spot Mr. Gerhardt coming in from the side of the room and hanging back to watch us.

A bunch of reporters' hands rise, but I signal for Jana to go first.

"Yes, Ahmed," she says, pointing at him.

"Nobody could score tonight. Would you say it's a fluke or is this something you're going to have to work on in practice?"

I move up to the microphone, but Jana twists it her way. "We'll be addressing it in practice for sure."

I exhale and she glares at me.

"Ted." She points at another reporter, and he stands.

"You guys are slipping every week in the standings. Do you think some of the opinions floating around out there are correct? That you two might just be in over your heads?"

Again, I shift my weight to answer, but Jana beats me to the microphone. "Neither one of us are in over our heads. Adjustments need to be made. That's all. Sometimes the best teams go through things like this. It will only make winning the Cup that much better." She's all smiles as if that can mask our problems.

Ted sits down looking unconvinced.

"Sasha," she says.

"Rumors say that the two of you barely talk. That Coach Burrows does his thing, and you do your own. Is that true? Are there problems on the inside?"

Jana looks at me sweetly but smugly at the same time,

and I have no idea what's going to come out of her mouth. "We don't always agree, but we're definitely a team on this."

More hands go up in the air.

"Tami," she says, and I inwardly groan. Didn't she learn her lesson last time?

"We've also heard whisperings that the two of you were involved."

"Not true. Who did you hear that from?" Jana shakes her head, too quick to dismiss Tami and her gossip. Jana has now probably convinced people it is, in fact, true.

"Last question. Nash." She points at him, and he smiles confidently.

I can tell just by looking at him, he knows something from the inside and he's about to test us on it.

"Since Miss Gerhardt is answering all the questions this evening, I was wondering how you're handling Maksim Petrov's groin injury? Will you be looking to bring another defenseman on to replace him before trade deadlines?"

Jana's mouth falls open and she glances at me, a clear giveaway she didn't know anything about it.

I slide up to the microphone. "As you saw tonight, Maksim is still playing. We're keeping an eye on things and constantly reassessing. As far as trades, it's way too early to talk about those at this point." I stand. "Thank you." I step aside to let Jana out before me.

Once we're in the hallway, she turns around and I'm surprised there's not actual steam coming out of her ears.

"How could you not tell me?"

I walk toward the locker room. "Give me a break, Jana. You don't want to know anything that happens with this team. All you want are the wins. You don't care about any of us." I mentally chastise myself for using the word us rather than players.

She takes my arm and swivels me around. "Don't make this about you. You're the one who told me to stay out of what happens on the ice."

"I told you not to question my coaching decisions, not desert your players. This entire season, you've been worrying more about what damn uniforms they wear than them coming together as a team."

"An injured player is something you should've come up to the office and told me. That is your responsibility." She pokes me in the chest.

I lean in close and lower my voice. "I went up there last night and you were gone for the evening. I didn't want to interrupt your date, so I figured if Maksim could play, then that settled it. And he did play. I have no idea how Nash figured out how he injured his groin."

She rises on her tiptoes to come closer to being eye to eye with me. "I wasn't on a date, and so what? Because you're jealous, you don't tell me things, try to sabotage me?"

I give a caustic laugh. "Jealous? You're the one who called out the Make-A-Wish mom as my date. Exactly who's the jealous one?"

The locker room doors open, and Aiden comes out with Cory. They're dressed and about to go to talk to the press.

"Mom and Dad, please stop fighting," Aiden says.

I flip them off while Jana completely ignores them.

"I wasn't jealous. I thought it was in bad taste. And why were you flirting with the Make-A-Wish mommy anyway?"

"I wasn't flirting. I was talking."

She rolls her eyes. "Whatever, like I care."

A door slams at the end of the hallway, startling us both, and we turn to find Mr. Gerhardt standing there.

"You two!" He points at us. "In my office. Now!"

We both huff out a breath.

"You mean my office?"

Jana really can't help herself, can she?

"Careful, I might just take that office back." He turns and heads back through the door he came from.

"Look what you did!" She narrows her eyes at me. "You got us in trouble."

"What are you, ten?"

Her fists clench on either side of her body and she groans. "You're so... just... uggghhh!"

She walks ahead first, and I follow her through the hallways to the elevator that will take us to the offices. There're still a few stragglers taking their time leaving the arena and I hear them voicing their displeasure about my coaching, the players, and the entire Fury organization.

"I knew it would be like this when Gerhardt let his daughter take over. What a joke. All these years and we're gonna lose the Cup again," one fan says.

"They can still turn it around. I bet they do."

"Are you kidding me? Did you see Petrov? He's the entire reason we lost. He couldn't run defense tonight to save his life."

Being a player, I'm used to the criticism. The way they're your biggest fans when you're playing well and your worst enemies when you're not.

"And what the hell was with Burrows? Get rid of McIntosh and put Burrows back in the net. The kid is useless. I knew it when they drafted him."

Jana doesn't turn around, as if she doesn't hear them, but it's impossible not to.

"It's the chick, I tell you. Rich trust fund girl. Her daddy gives her a team to make his little girl happy. I call bullshit. They have a responsibility to us."

I wince. That was harsh.

"If she worried about wins half as much as she worries about their damn uniforms, maybe we'd be somewhere. I saw her on that *News Today* show talking about the retro uniforms. Who the hell gives a shit about those if you aren't winning?"

Jana's shoulders falter, but she'll never let me know how much hearing those insults affect her. That might actually make her vulnerable and Lord knows there's nothing worse to Jana Gerhardt than that.

"Just go to the country club, sweetheart, and find yourself a rich husband, pop a few kids out to make daddy happy." Both the fans laugh.

Finally, we press the button for the elevator that will take us up to the executive offices. Once we're secure inside the small space, I decide I can't let those words go.

"They're just angry. People aren't on our side when we lose. You can't let them get to you."

She straightens her shoulders. "I'm not. I know that."

But there was a hitch in her tone, so I run my thumb over the inside of her wrist. "Jana, they're just assholes."

A tear slips down, but she turns away from me, quickly brushing it away. "I'm fine, Kane." She slides her arm out of my hold and walks out of the elevator.

My stomach clenches at the sight of that tear and her refusal to take any comfort from me. For the millionth time, I wonder what it will take for her to tear down the wall she's built around herself. I fear I'll never be able to climb or crack it.

CHAPTER 10

Jana

My dad is waiting in my new office—his old one—looking around. The fact he still has a key is a reminder that my position very well may be temporary.

Kane walks in behind me, but my dad is busy inspecting the space and doesn't address us right away. The room looks completely different. The furniture is either all white or a light wood. Gold and black accents permeate the space.

"It's definitely you," my dad says, sitting behind *my* desk. "Have a seat, you two."

I fold myself into one of the guest chairs I didn't think I'd ever be sitting in. I'm a fool for not realizing my dad would tug this away from me. Kane sits next to me and the energy coming off him is so strong, I'm desperate to agree to whatever my dad says just to get out of here.

"I like to think I'm a patient guy," my dad says, leaning back in my chair before remembering it's not his enormous chair anymore. "You've had months to figure this out together, and disappointed doesn't even begin to convey how I feel about this situation." He rises out of the chair and comes around the desk to pace behind us. Neither of us turns toward him. "There's no camaraderie, no team, no chemistry between you two or out on that ice with the players."

"Dad, I—"

He's quick to stop me. "I heard you never had a team outing this season."

"I—"

"It's critical to start every season with a team-bonding event. The more they know one another, the more they work as a team toward the common goal. I realize there are friend groups within the team, but they *all* need to feel a part of things. Jana, you didn't even know one of your players was injured."

Kane raises his hand. "That's on me. I came up yesterday and Jana was busy. I should've sent her an email."

"Are you even having weekly meetings? Have either of you agreed on trades that might need to happen?"

"Well, we were—"

Again, Dad cuts me off. "I'll take that as a no." He rounds the desk and sits in my chair, his back straight, hands linked together. "Things change now."

I'm not sure Kane has ever heard the tone in my dad's voice right now, but I have. Many times, when I was an out-of-control teenager. Once I took five of my friends to New York City on his plane and his dime. I guess I deserved his wrath that time.

I feel myself closing up like I always do when my dad gets this way. My dad's going to tell me what needs to happen and I'm going to allow it because I'm a complete and utter failure at this job he entrusted to me.

"With all due respect—" Kane says.

"I'm sorry to interrupt you, Kane, but this is my show now. I bought this team when no one wanted hockey in Florida. I've nurtured it and thought I was leaving it in capable hands. I don't know why you two can't put your differences aside to run this team."

I open my mouth, but Dad raises his hand for me to stop.

"This is what we're going to do." He tears a piece of paper off the notepad sitting to his right and takes my favorite gold pen, the one Paisley got me when he gave me the position, and starts scribbling on the sheet. "First thing, we're planning a team-building event." He looks up. "And you will both attend. I can't be clearer that the players have to trust everyone in the organization, including the people in these offices."

I blow out a breath. I know the majority of them on a personal level.

"We're going to schedule weekly meetings between the two of you. You will be attending charity events either together, alone, or with a date, I don't really care. But you both need to be at them to represent the organization, together. You two will be doing every press conference together, and Jana, you will attend every away game."

"Um... you never attended away games?"

"Because I had a family. I went to the games I could. Since you're single, I'm not sure what else you have to do that doesn't involve this team."

"Dad, this isn't how other teams work."

He drops my pen. "I've never managed this team like every other team. I've made it clear what I want at the end of this. I want the Fury to win the Cup. I've set the both of you up to make that happen, and so far, you're messing it up."

"Mr. Gerhardt, I think I speak for both of us when I say that we never meant for this to happen. It just kind of spiraled and..."

Without openly telling my dad what was going on with

us before our promotions, we don't really have a valid argument.

My dad studies us for a moment. "Charlotte has her theories about you two. Is she right?"

My forehead wrinkles. "Mom has a theory? Doesn't matter." I shake my head. "I'm sure she's wrong."

"So you two aren't involved in some type of casual sexual relationship?"

My eyes widen for a second before I recover.

Kane coughs. "Sorry, saliva went down the wrong way." He thumps himself on the chest.

"No, Dad, we're not."

"Then I don't see what the problem is. So tonight, you're going to go to dinner together. Not Carmelo's. Somewhere, preferably where cameras are, so everyone can see the two of you kissed and made up after that disaster of a press conference." He slides the paper over to us, and I pick it up as though I won't remember what he's demanding of us.

"So pretty much we're stuck side by side until we win the Cup?" Kane asks.

My dad nods without any trace of a smile.

I know better than to argue with my dad. He's not going to change his mind. I take the piece of paper and stand.

"Hang on, sweetie."

Kane glances at me, looking uneasy, and I sit, dodging eye contact.

"I put you both in the positions you're in because I know you can do this. You just need a little teamwork. And once we get the team aligned, success will come." He pulls out his wallet. "Dinner's on me tonight."

Kane raises his hand. "There's no need for that, Mr. Gerhardt. I can take care of the dinner bill."

"We can both take care of the dinner bill," I say. I don't want Kane thinking this is some kind of date or something.

Kane groans as if I'm this annoying teenager who can't stop back talking.

"No. No. This one is on me." Dad passes over five one-hundred-dollar bills.

"We don't need that much," Kane says. "We can happily share a meal at McDonald's."

My dad laughs, probably thinking Kane is joking. But at this point with us, I wouldn't be surprised if Kane took us through the drive-through and we ate in front of my house so he could get rid of me faster.

"I'm hoping this is the last time I need to intervene this season." My dad stands and takes a moment to look around. "I like the way the office looks, sweetie." He clasps Kane on the shoulder as though he's his son or something, then Dad's gone.

Kane turns to me as the door clicks shut. "So?"

"Taco Bell sounds excellent." I stand and grab my belongings off my coat hook.

"Are you sure you want pictures of yourself eating a burrito? He said he wants us to be seen."

I growl in annoyance. "Then there's only one place."

He nods, knowing if it's not Carmelo's—where all the Fury players go—it's the steak house next door, which has the slowest service ever.

"We probably can't get in this late."

"Oh, we can get in." He pulls out his phone and walks out to the hallway.

I take a moment to admire the way the suit fits Kane's body perfectly. If my dad is going to force us together, I have to have my guard up if I stand a chance of not sleeping with him again.

Twenty minutes later, we're sitting at a booth in Gino's Steak House. The same guy owns Gino's and Carmelo's, except Gino's is fancy. The owner, Vinny, loves the Florida Fury, said he grew up in New York playing hockey before moving down here to open a few restaurants and live a slower-paced life.

The fact he comes to our table to open our bottle of wine right after we order explains how Kane got us in. "Coach now, huh? You haven't been in in a while."

Kane plays with the ends of his silverware. "Not much to celebrate."

Vinny doesn't say much but gives a face to suggest our team isn't in the worst shape ever. Which is true, but our team should have way more wins than losses. "And, Miss Gerhardt, nice to see you again. How is your father?"

"He's good, Vinny. Enjoying retirement."

Kane scoffs because that's not true.

Vinny gets the wine bottle opened and pours Kane a taste.

"She's way pickier than me." Kane nods in my direction.

"Of course, ladies first."

Instead of doing the entire swirling and smelling before tasting thing like I've been taught my entire life, I sip the wine and nod for him to go ahead and pour two glasses. "It's excellent, Vinny."

"Enjoy your meal. I'll check in at dessert." He winks and walks to the next table, greeting the guests by name.

I twirl the stem of my glass, watching the red wine swirl around the large glass.

"Maybe we need some ground rules," Kane says.

I look up from my wine. "Ground rules?"

"Rules to make sure lines don't blur. You were right when you said things would be too complicated if we continued sleeping together. But we've tried for months to stay away from one another. Obviously that ruined the team dynamic, so we're gonna have to be around one another now. We'll put rules in place."

"As in?"

"For the team-building retreat, we stay on opposite sides of the hotel. And for the weekly meetings, we have them in public places. For the press conferences, we'll have a player join us each week."

I laugh. "I don't need to put rules in place so I don't sleep with you. I hate to break it to you, but you're not that irresistible." I swear, the ego on this man.

I ignore the niggling in my subconscious telling me he has a point.

"I'm just trying to make it easier. Not just the sexual tension—"

"There's sexual tension?"

He quirks an eyebrow.

"Have you not noticed that we don't even get along, Kane?"

"That's just our way of getting under each other's skin. You know as well as I do there's nothing we love more than to fight and then fuck. Stop denying it, Jana."

I gulp a large sip of my wine. "Well, we're done with the fucking, and the entire reason my dad called us in was because of our fighting."

He leans back in the booth, his long arms extending across the table, fiddling with his own wineglass stem. "Okay, so you have no feelings for me?"

"Nope," I say, popping the *p*.

"You don't want to have sex with me right now?"

"God, no!" I catch myself before my voice rises too high.

"All right, let's up the ante a little then."

"What are you talking about?" I sip my wine to distract myself from the fact that I am lying directly to this man's face.

"Weekly meetings at my house, I cook you dinner. Team building, we're on the same team. Press conferences are just you and me and a drink afterward." His cocky smirk is back on display, and I hate to admit that I've kind of missed it.

"That sounds a lot like dating, and I don't want to date you, remember?" I grab a roll from the basket and take a bite, needing something in my stomach.

"It's two coworkers having a relationship that will better the team."

"This is so stupid and childish. You have to make everything a competition. I have nothing to prove." I roll my eyes.

He chuckles. "I guess we'll see about that." He gives me a challenging stare, and damn my ego because I can't not want to show him how wrong he is.

"Okay, I'm all in."

He sips his wine, his copper eyes with flecks of green locking with mine over the rim of his glass.

Whatever. I so have this. And maybe if I keep telling myself that, I'll start to believe it.

CHAPTER 11

"It's the classic, cliché story."

Kane

I throw Rocky's ball toward the edge of the water, and he chases it. He's a Collie mix I rescued a couple of years ago and is always up for a game of fetch. I turn and poke at the firepit that's right off my backyard on the beach, then go back to my flatiron grill on the deck where I'm preparing shrimp, veggies, and noodles.

"I swear, sometimes, Kane Burrows..." Jana appears around the corner from the front of the house.

"You got my note." I smile bright, but I get a scowl in return.

"If I'd known I was going hiking, I'd have worn better shoes. Ever hear of a landscaper?"

"Sorry about that. Coaching is so different than playing. I used to have time to do all that myself." I flip the shrimp. "Lucky for you, dinner is almost ready."

"Good. The sooner we're done, the sooner I can get out of here." She looks at my patio furniture with surprise and sits down.

"Not what you expected?"

She shrugs. "I don't have a lot of expectations when it comes to you."

I smile to myself then spear a piece of the broccoli and

hold the fork out in front of her mouth. She shakes her head.

"Come on," I urge her.

She finally opens, and I slide the fork into that mouth I love so much. She moans, chewing and swallowing. "What kind of seasoning is that?"

I select my own piece and toss it in the air, catching it in my mouth. "My own special seasoning." I wink.

"Well, it's surprisingly good."

"Surprisingly, huh?"

"You are a bachelor. I didn't think you cooked much since you've never invited me over."

I chuckle. "Because you liked things on your turf, and since it was just sex, I figured who cares where we had it."

"Can we not talk about it anymore? Since that's over."

I put the meal I've prepared on a serving dish. "Just want to forget it happened?"

"Yes, please," she says, then looks up at me as though she can't believe she said it out loud.

"Fine. We'll forget the fact that I've seen you naked and know you like it when I tie you to the bed."

"Seriously?" she scoffs.

I give her a cocky grin just to piss her off. She's way too on edge these days.

"Look who I found at my back door, seeing if his girl-friend can play." My next-door neighbor Emma walks up on the desk with Rocky next to her.

It takes him two seconds to see the new face and he jets toward Jana.

"No, Rocky," I say, grabbing for his collar while balancing the dish on the palm of my other hand.

When I finally get both things to stop moving, Rocky

gives another tug because he loves new people. The serving tray wobbles and ends up face down on my patio. *Damn it.*

"I'm sorry," Emma says. "I didn't know you had company."

"It's okay." I let go of Rocky to pick up the mess. He rushes over to Jana, puts both paws on her shoulders, and licks her face.

"Um... Kane?" Her voice has a definite note of panic.

"Shit." I leave the mess and grab Rocky. "Sit, Rocky."

He does what I say, but his tail is wagging a mile a minute.

Jana runs the back of her hand down her face where Rocky left his saliva and coughs what I think might be bile rushing up her throat. She stands. "If you'll excuse me. Do you have a bathroom?"

"Yeah, inside to the right." I motion toward the patio doors.

When Jana shuts the French door, I glance at Emma. "He hasn't been like that since he met you."

Emma laughs. "And thank goodness I'm a dog person. I'm not so sure she is though."

"No. At least not one the size of Rocky." I pet Rocky's head. "What got into you, buddy?"

Emma grabs a piece of zucchini I left on the grill by mistake and pops it into her mouth. "I'd say that it's that she's so hot and even though you neutered the poor thing, he still gets horny just like his daddy."

I shake my head at her. "Where's Sam tonight?"

"Working. She's on call. I was going to swindle my way into an invitation over here, but I see you've got plans." She wiggles her eyebrows.

"She's my boss."

"Oh, that's her?" She peeks in through the window, but

there's no sign of Jana. She probably sneaked out the front door.

"Yeah."

"She fits the bill. Not that I shop where she does, but her outfit looks expensive. And then there's all that gold she's wearing." Emma looks down at her paint-covered cutoff jean shorts and tank top.

While her partner, Sam, is a doctor, Emma's a painter and owns a small gallery in the downtown area. Rocky is their dog Penny's boyfriend. We're one big happy family on this side of the city.

The French door opens, and Emma stands. I throw all the food in my outside garbage can.

"I guess it's pizza for us," I tell Jana.

Rocky walks up to her, calmer now, but his tail could leave whip marks it's moving so fast. Jana hesitantly pats his head. Rocky sits and scoots closer to her, and Jana pets him again.

"I better get going," Emma says. "I've been procrastinating on this piece, and it's supposed to be the center focus at the gallery next week."

"You're an artist?" Jana asks. "What gallery?"

"Sorry. Jana Gerhardt, this is Emma Hayes. Emma, Jana." Emma walks over and shakes Jana's hand.

"Nice to meet you," Jana says.

"You too. The gallery is on the corner of Main and Sunset. It's just a small place because Sam insisted I show my art, so..."

"So now your paintings are all over the area. People go mad over her stuff," I tell Jana.

Emma's cheeks redden. "He's being kind. You two have a great night." She looks at where Rocky has his head on Jana's lap. "Do you want me to take Rocky for the night? I'm sure Penny won't mind." She looks at Jana. "Penny is our dog. Rocky's girlfriend, or so he thinks. Imagine your welcome from him but more dry humping. That's how he says hello to Penny."

"Sounds like his dad," Jana says.

Emma cracks up. "I guess they witness it long enough, they start to mimic. And here we are, not praising Rocky for doing what his master teaches."

"Bye, Emma." I push at her shoulder.

She laughs. "Nice to meet you, Jana. Have a great night, you two."

"I'll check out your gallery sometime. I'm always looking for new artists."

"Emma Hayes Gallery. Nothing original." Emma waves and gives me an expression to say good luck with that one.

"Sorry about the meal." I face Jana, who's stiff as a board with the dog a mere inch away. "Rocky." I clap my hands, but he doesn't move. I pick up his ball and throw it out to the beach, and he still doesn't move. "I guess you're taking him home."

I go into the house and grab the take-out menus for nearby restaurants.

"Maybe we should just skip dinner and have our meeting." She turns slightly.

Rocky slides his ass along the patio to stay as close to her as he can. It's comical, but I'm trying not to laugh. He's got good taste. If Jana ever opened up and allowed me in, I'd be doing the exact thing.

"No. I'm feeding you. Close your eyes."

"What? Why?" It's not surprising that she doesn't just do as I ask.

"C'mon, do it."

She huffs but closes her eyes. I grab her hand and manipulate her fingers so that her pointer finger is out.

I spread out the menus in front of her. "You're going to pick without looking and that's where we'll eat."

"I'd rather just decide."

"That's no fun. We're doing it this way. Unless you're one of those picky eaters who will just complain."

She peeks one eye open. "Stop trying to bait me. I'm here at your place, eating dinner with you, and your dog won't leave me alone. I think I deserve some props."

I smile because she's right. I know if she had her choice, she wouldn't be here, but she is, and she's being a fairly decent sport. When I suggested we get together at my place, I never considered how great she'd look among my things and my dog. That she could seem to fit here, in this small two-bedroom house that's not a mansion. There are no marble floors or elaborate chandeliers. My place couldn't be simpler. I'm the only person on our team who doesn't have a pool. But I like having her here. I wonder if it was a very bad idea to force her to come here.

I'm so busy admiring her on my back patio, it takes me a second to realize her finger is pressed on a menu. "Mexican, I guess."

"Margaritas to go?" she asks. "Extra salt on the rim."

"I can make you a margarita."

We open the menu and each figure out what we want, then I call in the order. Both of us decide on tacos and guacamole with chips.

"Come on in and I'll make you a margarita. I've got all the fixin's."

"I make the best margaritas." She follows me after I whistle at Rocky.

When we're in the kitchen, I pull out my blender, the margarita mix, tequila, and salt. My head is buried in the fridge, looking for the limes, until I look over my shoulder and see she must've grabbed them while I was assembling the other ingredients. She has them on a cutting board already.

I'd be lying if I said the idea of Jana making herself at home in my space isn't like a shot of warmth to my chest.

"You have to run the lime around the edge. Do you have a plate?" she asks.

I lean my back on the fridge and watch her, not bothering to answer. This is a woman who's probably had more drinks made for her than those she's made for herself in her lifetime. She notices me watching, and I catch the slightest pink tinge invade her cheeks. I'm already half chub in my shorts because as usual, I want her. It's so unfair—since I've already had her, I know exactly what I'm missing and she's not mine to have anymore. But damn it, she really looks good in my space.

"Are you going to help?" It's not a question but more of a demand.

I push off the fridge and come to stand beside her. "I was letting you prove your worth."

She hip checks me playfully, and finally it feels as though the bulletproof glass she's put up between us fractures a bit. "Just mix the drink. I'm in desperate need of alcohol after this week and my dad."

I pour the mix, tequila, and ice in the blender. "It must've been hard to grow up with such a successful dad."

I saw her demeanor that night her dad gave us hell for dropping the ball. She was closed up—even more than usual—and looked like disappointing him made her feel about two feet tall. I can't relate since my dad died when I was still pretty young. After that, my mom didn't invest much emotionally in either my brother or me.

She huffs. "The only thing hard about it is that I'm an only child, and I wasn't born with a penis."

I don't say anything, hoping she continues. The tightness in my chest eases when she does.

"It's the classic, cliché story. Powerful and successful man wants an heir but gets his little princess instead. But rather than teach his little girl about fairy tales where the prince comes to save the day on his white horse, he teaches her to ride the white horse herself. But she can never quite live up to what the prince might have done."

I walk over to the cupboard, grab a plate, and set it in front of her. "I'd want my own daughter to think the same thing. I wouldn't want her to rely on a man." That is, if I had a daughter, which I won't since I'll never have kids.

"I'm appreciative of it. I know what my reputation is, but I'd rather that than be some doormat for some guy to trample all over. But there's always that one small piece of my dad that only sees my gender. He'd never admit it, but he's old school at heart and always worries I'll make decisions based on emotions and not facts."

I pour our margaritas into the glasses she's prepared with heavy salt rims. "I think emotions have to be considered in some decisions."

"Maybe that's why we're here right now. Maybe that's the reason the Fury isn't succeeding."

I shake my head. "I don't think that's it at all."

She sips her margarita, and her shoulders fall in relaxation. "Not much I can do to change things. You can't turn back time and change how you were raised."

Isn't that the truth.

CHAPTER 12

"You can't do that."

Jana

I'm walking out of my office when Barbara hands me a handwritten note.

"Have a great night, Barbara. Are you coming to the game?"

"No, I have to get home. Have fun."

I'm kind of getting used to Barbara's notes, except for the fact that I read them, stuff them in a pocket or in my purse, and forget them entirely. I read the one in my hand.

Kane Burrows called and said his brother, Lee, is going to attend the game. FYI since he's the quarterback for the San Francisco Kingsmen.

Kane's brother is a professional football player? How did I not know this?

I dial up Kane on my way to the elevator, hoping that he's not too busy with his pregame routine.

"I take it Barbara just gave you my message?" he says by way of answering. There's the humor in his tone that I've missed during the last few months of us being at odds.

"How did I not know your brother is the quarterback for the Kingsmen? Your parents must be over the moon at having two sons who are professional athletes. I didn't even know you had a brother."

"I guess. My dad's dead."

Foot, meet mouth.

I cringe. "I'm sorry." The elevator arrives, but I wait so my phone won't drop the call.

"Don't be. It was a long time ago. But you're right, he would be proud. Two Canadians playing down in the US. You haven't made it until you've made it in America." I can hear the humor in his voice.

I giggle at his way of throwing that in there. "How about I bring him up to the suite? We're retiring Brock Allen's number in a ceremony before the game tonight so I'll be down at the ice for that, but then I'll be bringing him, his wife Kelsey and their kids up to join me in the box."

"No. He's fine on the floor. I just figured you might want to tell the cameras to be on the lookout or something. It's good publicity."

"Thinking of all the angles, huh?"

"Anything to get the heat off of my coaching. The chat rooms are horrible."

I haven't had the guts to read what the chat groups say about me. Hearing those fans the other week was enough to make me want to crawl into a hole.

"Let's bring him up to the suite. Dad would probably insist on it," I say.

"I'm not sure. He's different than me."

My brow furrows. "How so?"

There's a long beat of silence. "I'm not sure... maybe more charismatic?"

"You mean he's not a grumpy, brooding man with an ego the size of China?"

He chuckles lightly. "Oh, he's got the ego. That's what happens when you don't have any responsibilities growing up. You get the ego, but you don't get jaded."

"Are you giving me a sliver of insight into how you grew up?"

"Believe me, if my brother has his way, you'll know everything about how we grew up by the end of the third period." He groans.

"All the more reason to invite him to the suite." I laugh and press the button for the elevator again. "Good luck tonight. I'll see you after for the press conference. Your brother's ticket will be at will call."

"We're playing Oregon," Kane says. "Tell me you have some lucky charm or superstition that will help us win tonight."

"Sure, I wear a special pair of panties every game. Come on. You know me better than that."

"If we win tonight, will you wear those panties every game after?"

"Um... no. You play back-to-back games."

"It's not like I said you couldn't wash them."

"My panties—" One of the women who works here waves to me on her way to the restroom, so I lower my voice. "My panties have nothing to do with winning games."

"I know." He laughs. "I was just hoping you'd tell me what panties you're wearing. Lacy or sheer? My favorite pair was those sheer dark-purple ones with the small bow in the middle."

My body heats with the memory of him using his teeth to drag them off me. How his eyes blazed with desire the first time I wore them for him.

"I'm wearing white cotton granny panties." I try to keep my voice even, so he won't know how much he still affects me.

"Damn, you just dumped a bucket of cold water over me.

Although at this point, I'd take you in those without complaint."

"Kane, we don't have that kind of relationship anymore." There's zero censure in my voice. In fact, I think I probably sound more disappointed than anything.

A long silence follows. "A man can dream. See you at the press conference, lady boss."

He ends the call and I step into the elevator, still over-heated from his words.

———

Lee Burrows is as tall as his brother, with the same dark hair although his is shorter, and he has no beard. Even though he's close to my age—thanks, Google—he doesn't seem as manly as Kane. Not in a bad way. The guy is a panty dropper for sure. But comparing the two of them in my mind makes me realize how much I prefer Kane's big, burly presence. The chin-length hair and full beard, the small crow's-feet at the corner of his eyes and his gruff demeanor, rather than his brother's charismatic charm.

"How did you get into football when your brother was playing hockey?" I ask Lee while we watch the game from the suite.

Currently, we're winning 2–0, and my dad won't stop bragging. I keep reminding him we have one more period before it's final. Anything can happen.

"I'm not sure. Kane's always played hockey. It was our dad's sport too. I never took to it. I was like a baby deer on the ice when Kane would try to play pond hockey with me as a kid. But the first time I got a football in my hand, something clicked for me."

I nod. "Maybe it's better. That way you didn't have to compete with each other."

Lee chuckles. "Kane was playing professionally before I was a teenager, so we weren't ever in the same stages of life at the same time. He got fortunate that he was able to play for the local WHL team and his career took off from there. If he'd had to be billeted somewhere and go play for another team, he probably wouldn't be playing right now."

"Why's that?" I sip my wine and take a cheese and cracker from one of the catering plates because I've barely eaten all day.

"To take care of us."

A small frown mars my face. "Us? Do you have more siblings?"

He chuckles and it sounds just like Kane's. "You ask a lot of questions. Let me squeeze one in?"

I nod. "Okay."

"Are you dating my brother?"

I glance at the ice where Kane is standing behind the team, wearing a suit. He's barking an order to one of the players while pointing at something on a clipboard to Bill, the assistant coach. He's so intense, but it's that alpha inside that's always drawn me to him. Kane never apologizes for his rough exterior, but wears it with pride.

"No," I answer truthfully. "Just curious."

"Because he's tight lipped, right?" He picks up a cheese puff appetizer thing and drops it in his mouth. Chews and swallows.

"He tends to keep to himself."

Lee leans on the railing of the suite and the camera scans to him, putting his image on the Jumbotron. He doesn't look uncomfortable at all. Just raises his hand and flashes a boyish grin that instantly wins over the crowd. Two brothers with two completely opposite personalities. One brother seems to hold the weight of the world on his shoulders, while the other acts as if he doesn't have a care in the world.

"I'm gonna let him fill you in on what he wants you to know. But I'll tell you this... if there is something there between you two, he holds a lot in. Don't take it personally. He doesn't let anyone in, but I hope one day he'll find his person. If anyone deserves it, it's my brother."

"That's very brotherly of you."

He shrugs. "He raised me. The man will make one heck of a father someday. I hope he gets his chance."

I open my mouth to say something—I'm not even sure what—but shut it when we get interrupted by one of the Fury front office staff.

Finishing my wine, I ponder Lee's words and wonder about their mother. Where was she when this was all going down? It makes sense why Kane would want a family if his own family was dysfunctional—he wants a do-over. But a family is something I can't give him. I'm not made to be a wife and a mother. I'm built for boardrooms and takeovers, not Band-Aids and PTA volunteering.

At the end of the third period, the score is 2–1 and the Fury are the victors.

"Want to head down with me?" I ask Lee. "Your brother and I have to do the press conference, then you two can get into whatever trouble you have planned."

"Sure, I don't mind seeing my brother sweat in front of reporters." He laughs, and we walk down the hallway toward the elevators. After we step into the small space and I press the button for the ground floor, Lee touches my arm a bit hesitantly. "I just wanted to say, I probably misspoke earlier. I mean… Kane wouldn't like it that I told you what I did, so could we maybe keep that between us?"

I smile. "Sure."

"I just want the best for him, but I don't want to push him any further away than he already is."

I try to figure out what Lee's talking about but can't. "No worries. I won't say a word."

"Thanks." He smiles at me as the elevator doors open. "Give me a tour?"

"Sure thing."

I lead Lee around the training rooms and the locker rooms. Kane is already waiting outside the pressroom when we reach it.

"Hey, you two." Kane smiles at me.

For a moment, I feel as though I'm his, but I'm not and I need to remember that's a choice *I* made.

"Just giving your brother the tour. Is it weird? Like looking at a younger version of yourself?" I ask.

Kane shakes his head but seems amused. "He looks like my mom, and I look like my dad."

"Plus, you have those little gray strands in your beard." I point at the imaginary grays with a smile.

He runs his hand down his beard. "I do not."

I shrug. "Let's get this over with."

Kane holds the door open for me and I walk behind the table, taking my seat. Kane sits next to me, and his knee touches mine, but neither one of us moves. In our past press conferences, we would have separated more, but it feels nice to know we're more like a team now.

Lee leans along the wall. A few reporters obviously recognize him, looking over, then murmuring between themselves.

"Ted," I call to the first reporter.

"Nice win tonight, Coach. My question is for Jana. Rumors are that you're doing a team-building event during the next three-day break. Do you think it's a bad idea rather than letting your players rest?"

I lean forward. "Team building is critical to our organization. Making sure all the players learn to lean on one another is and will remain a priority."

"Wasn't it your dad who demanded it happen? Another rumor says your dad's stripped you of the owner position."

Kane leans toward the microphone, but I grab it and glare at him. He doesn't need to swoop in and save me. "I can say with certainty I am still the owner." More hands go up. "Ahmed."

"But aren't you only the owner because you're his daughter? You obviously failed at the job for the first few months. Doesn't the team building usually happen before the season begins?"

"Kane and I didn't think we could fit it in the schedule as quickly as we needed to with all the changes that had been made."

"Because you were more concerned about retro uniforms." Ahmed sits down as if it's a statement.

"Listen, can we stay on topic and discuss tonight's win?" I draw in a deep breath to ease the tension bunching my shoulders. I point at the last person I'm going to take a question from. "Tami."

Kane groans next to me, but she never criticizes me.

"Thanks, Jana. I love your blouse."

I smile. "Thank you."

"So, Kane, I see your brother is in town. Hi, Lee."

Lee gives her a small wave.

"Can you tell us where you'll be tonight? Is Lee staying

for a couple days? Is he interested in doing a bachelor auction?"

Kane leans forward, holding the microphone to his mouth, and clears his throat. "Tami, you know I'm not answering any of those questions."

She sits down and grins but shakes her head at him good-naturedly.

I'm ready to get out of here, but Kane continues talking. "As for the rest of the reporters here... if you're going to continue to take cheap shots at Jana or question what's happening behind closed doors, then she will no longer be in these press conferences. We're here to discuss the game, which we won, so you should be asking what made me switch out Warner for Tweetie or why'd I take McIntosh out in the third when the game was close. It shouldn't involve you throwing stones at a woman who's here every day, working her ass off to bring us the best team. This is the last time we're going to have this conversation. Do you all understand?"

There are a few nods, but I'm so embarrassed, I want to drag him out of this room.

Lee is clearly trying not to laugh.

We stand from the chairs and exit the room. As soon as we're out in the hallway, I whirl around.

"What the hell?" I shout at Kane. "You can't do that."

"What? They were being assholes and trying to bait you. They'd never say shit like that to a male owner."

"I can stick up for myself."

Aiden comes out of the locker room with Warner for their interviews, hair still damp. Lee says hello to them, and they stop to talk to him.

In the meantime, Kane drags me down the hallway. "I'm not gonna sit back and let them talk to you like that."

"You're not my prince," I seethe through gritted teeth. "Now I look weak."

"Jana, you could never look weak. You're the toughest woman I know. I'm sorry if it bothers you, but I'll never stand by and let them do that to you or any other woman. But especially not you."

Our eyes lock and my ire calms when I see his genuine honesty. As much as I hate what he did, I can't deny that it feels nice to have someone stick up for me.

"Come on, we're all going to dinner." Lee motions for us to continue down the hall.

"You two go. Have a good time." I give him a small smile.

Lee walks over and puts his arm around my shoulders. "Hell no. I see my brother act that protective over a woman, she's someone I need to get to know better."

Against my better judgment, I find myself going with them.

CHAPTER 13

"You really like her, huh?"

Kane

The last thing I want to do is go to dinner with Lee and Jana. Separately would've been fine, but together is gonna cause problems. Lee has a mouth on him, and what I think should be private, he never does.

So, Carmelo's it is, because my hope is that the other guys will keep Lee busy and maybe I can score some alone time with Jana.

Drake and Langley were still in the pressroom when we left, so we're not the last to arrive.

"Did you tell Paisley to come?" I ask Jana when I spot Paisley in a booth. Ever since the pregnancy announcement, neither she nor Maksim have been going out after the game. Then again, tonight was a big win.

"She's my ride or die. Pregnant or not."

I can't help but wonder if she wants Paisley here to act as a buffer between us.

In the past few weeks since Jana and I have had to spend more time together, it feels as though her animosity toward me is dwindling. We have normal conversations, her scowls are rarer, and sometimes she even laughs. I don't hate it.

I slide into the round booth with Maksim, Paisley, Tweetie, and Tedi, but Jana says she's heading to the bathroom. Tedi and Paisley say they'll join her.

Brielle, our normal waitress, comes over to take our drink orders. Lee orders the calamari appetizer.

I lean in so I can speak to him without Maksim and Tweetie hearing. "Cool it on any information pertaining to our homelife."

Lee smirks, knowing all too well how tight a hold I keep on our family secrets. He should too. I'm sure he doesn't want to be known as having a hermit mom who can't take care of herself ever since her husband died.

"I mean it."

He raises both hands. "Fine. Does she even know you're from Canada?"

Sometimes my brother is stupid as shit, and I give him a look to say just that. He chuckles because he always just fucking chuckles as though he doesn't have a care in the world.

"I'll take that expression as a yes," he says.

Jana and the girls come out of the bathroom a few minutes later. I'm impressed she didn't need a longer pep talk to sit through a dinner with my brother and me. She slides into the booth, and Brielle brings over a glass of wine and two beers.

"You really should get one of these seltzers." Tedi holds up the can to show Jana.

Brielle stops and looks at Jana with a questioning expression.

"Sure," Jana says with a shrug.

"Girls and their drinks," Lee says, laughing.

My brother has no idea who he's sitting at this table with. But he will in a minute.

"Excuse me?" Jana sips her wine, her lipstick smudged on the glass when she pulls it away.

I close my eyes for a moment to rip away the vision of

that lipstick on my dick not that long ago. But it's hard to ignore, because it's absolutely a core memory at this point.

"Just sayin'. Guys have shots of whiskey and girls drink those things." He points at the can that Brielle puts down on the table, along with a glass. Does she know her clientele or what?

"This is my favorite flavor," Brielle tells Jana.

Jana smiles and nods in thanks to her, then returns her attention to my brother. "What are you suggesting, Lee?"

Jana sounds innocent enough, but I know she's ready to fight if she needs to. My poor baby brother is clueless to what he's started. I sit back and smile, watching the show.

Lee nods for Brielle's attention. "Seven shots of whiskey."

"Seven? Paisley is pregnant and I'm not drinking whiskey." Jana pours her drink into the glass.

"Exactly my point." Lee gives her a cocky grin.

She rolls her eyes. "I *can* drink whiskey. I'm *choosing* not to. And have you ever thought that maybe you drink that because of what society has conditioned you to think is appropriate for a guy to drink? You'd probably prefer my fruity-flavored seltzer if you gave it a try."

She slides the can across the table. Lee picks it up, and pretends it's a fine wine, smelling, swirling, then sloshing it in his mouth. Smart-ass.

"It's good on a hot day maybe, but let's be honest, I'm Canadian. I need something that keeps the blood warm on cold nights."

Jana nods. "Now that makes sense. You want the burn in your chest and the warmth in your veins. So don't give me all that bullshit about women's drinks and men's drinks."

Lee chuckles and looks at me from the corner of his eye. "How many fights do you guys get into in a week?"

"Pretty much every day," I answer truthfully.

"No," Jana interrupts. "We don't fight every day."

I tilt my head because my memory says yes.

"We just see things differently. That's all. It's not a fight," Jana tells Lee.

"Believe me, we don't see things the same either." He waves his finger between the two of us.

"You guys are so opposite. How did your mom raise you guys to be so different?" Jana takes a hefty gulp of her drink, waiting for one of us to answer.

"My mom was too—"

I interrupt my brother. "She had to work all the time, so we were on our own a lot."

"I was never alone," Jana says with a sigh. "Either it was my parents, a nanny, or a housekeeper."

"Life of the rich and famous." Lee passes out shot glasses to everyone except Paisley, then raises his in the air.

"You don't have to drink it," I tell Jana, but she picks up her shot glass and clinks it with Lee's.

"To the Fury!" Lee says.

We clink again and down the shots. Jana impresses me by taking it all in one shot.

The calamari comes shortly after, and Lee eats the majority of it himself. Jana asks for another seltzer while I'm only halfway done with my beer.

Lee leans toward Jana as though he's keeping a secret. "So, nothing's going on with you two? Really?"

Jana looks at me. I can already see her cheeks are a little pink and she's wearing the smile she does when she's getting buzzed. "Nope." She pops the *p*, and I'm thankful she didn't say anything else because I don't need my brother in my business.

Drake, Saige, Ford, Lena, and a few other players trickle

in. Even Warner and Imogen make an appearance to celebrate beating Oregon's ass. I have to admit, it feels good after them beating us earlier in the season.

Drinks keep arriving at the table and I'm not even sure who's ordering them. At one point I have three shots in front of me that I don't drink because I feel a responsibility to look out for Jana. She'd absolutely hate that if I ever told her that's how I feel, but tough shit. She's on her fourth seltzer before I realize she's laughing manically. Not Jana at all.

"She's fun," Lee says before he heads to the dance floor where a lot of the girls are dancing with each other.

A few guys slide in next to me, congratulating me on the win. Saying encouraging things about how they knew I could do it and some other bullshit. It was all them. They've worked their asses off for me.

One by one, they join their girls on the dance floor while a few puck bunnies keep my brother busy, probably recognizing him. A redhead keeps trying to make eye contact with me, and when I don't make a move, she slowly walks toward me. I've been down this road before, and I have to decide right now what I'm going to do—tell her straight up I'm not interested, be polite but withdrawn, or spend the night chatting with her knowing nothing will come of it.

Jana whips around on the dance floor and heads in my direction, accidentally and unknowingly blocking the girl. She stands at the end of the booth with her hand out. "Come on and dance. Celebrate with everyone."

"We haven't won anything."

"We beat Oregon and that's enough. For tonight." She crawls on the bench seat on her knees and meets me in the center of the booth.

"How many of those have you had?" I nod at the can in her hand.

She looks at it and shrugs. "The girls did a few shots. God, it feels good to not worry about anything for a moment. You should try it."

"One of us should be sober."

"Come," she says, disregarding what I said.

"I don't really dance."

"'I don't really dance.'" She mocks me with a deep voice as if that's how I sound. "Everyone dances. You don't have to be good. You just enjoy yourself. Have fun." She gets a hold of my hand, mostly because I let her. Because I have a soft spot for her, as stupid as that makes me feel sometimes. "Your hands are so big."

I nod, looking at her delicate fingers adorned with rings, but none of them of any significance like a wedding or engagement ring. For a moment, I wonder what kind of engagement ring she'd like. Gold? Platinum? All diamonds? She seems like the vintage type, but I'm not sure. Or why the hell I'm even thinking of this either.

"You know what they say about big hands."

She giggles and tugs on my hand, my arm pulling away from my side. "It's big feet. C'mon."

"One dance," I mumble.

The dance floor is packed and it's almost all Fury players, their girls, and random puck bunnies. Jana wraps her arms around my neck and sways her delicious hips to the beat.

Tedi puts her arms around both of us, although she can't reach my shoulders. "I love seeing this. Go home and get some." She smacks both of our asses.

I shake my head and look around the dance floor until I find who I'm looking for. "Tweetie?" I nod at his girlfriend.

"Got her." He comes over and diverts Tedi away.

The music changes to a slow song. I'm about to leave, but Jana tightens her hold on me.

"One dance," she whispers into my ear. "Just one."

Something about the way she asks makes it so I can't say no.

I stand in place and our bodies sway to "Strangers" by Maddie & Tae. She rests her head on my chest, and I inhale the scent of her shampoo. The same scent that would cover my skin after a night spent with her.

Having my hands on her feels so right. I hate that I close my eyes for a moment and wonder what it would be like if she really was mine. She's always pushing me away, and right now, it almost feels as though she's offering herself up to me. I want to take her up on it more, I realize, than I've wanted anything in a long time. But not when she's been drinking.

The lyrics of the song ring true, because although there's so much Jana doesn't know about my past, she's the only one I feel truly knows me. Who I am on the inside. What I'm thinking most times. Where I'm coming from.

As the song winds down, I tighten my arms around her, not wanting it to end. She draws back and looks up at me. My dick twitches when it registers the lust filling her eyes. Her hand falls in mine and she turns us toward the hallway that leads to the bathrooms. She tucks us into the dark hallway and presses my back to the wall. My hands grip her hips, wishing we were somewhere private.

"Kiss me." She licks her plump lips.

My cock strains the confines of my dress pants. Her words are the ones I've wanted to hear since she cut me off months ago. I bend down, ready to taste her again, but she loses her equilibrium and stumbles to the side.

It's the reminder I needed that she's drunk.

I shake my head, and she frowns. "Not here. Not tonight."

"Come on. You know you want to." She grips my biceps and leans into me.

The press of her ample tits against my hard flesh makes my voice waver. "Want isn't the issue. You're drunk."

"I was drinking seltzers. They're like wine coolers." She straightens up, licks her lips, and runs her finger down my chest and past my waistline.

I'm not surprised when she grabs my dick and applies the slightest pressure. I suck in a breath. It feels fucking fantastic to have her hands on me again.

"Jesus, Jana. We can't." I grip her wrist.

"Why not? We did it before when we'd both been drinking."

"That was different, and you know it. Let me take you home. Get you to bed."

"No." She draws back and crosses her arms. "You're really denying me?"

"That's not what I'm doing. I'm just not going to take advantage of you."

Annoyance flashes across her face. I prepare for the lashing she's probably going to give me, but the minute she points her finger at my chest, her head circles as if it's grown too heavy for her to hold up and she falls into me. I catch her, then pick her up over my shoulder.

Grabbing my cell phone from my pocket, I arrange for an Uber and tell them to meet me in the back. I text my brother to meet me by the back door with her purse. He shows up five minutes later.

"Whoa, what happened? She's a lightweight, huh?" He opens the back door.

"Let's just get her home."

"You really like her, huh?"

He gets in the front of the car, and I sit in the back of the Uber with Jana's head in my lap. She looks so peaceful and relaxed.

"Why do you say that?" I ask without looking away from Jana's face.

"Because normally you'd have handed a woman off to her friends. Plus, I'm your brother. I know these things. You're not fooling anyone with the way you look at her."

I feel a line form at the bridge of my nose. "You have no idea what you're talking about."

"Everyone in there knows the two of you want each other."

"Says the man with four women hanging off him tonight."

He shrugs. "I'm on the market."

"So am I."

He laughs as though I just told the funniest fucking joke he's ever heard. "After what I witnessed tonight, I'd say you're very much *off* the market, big brother."

The Uber drives toward Jana's, and I stare at her long blonde hair in my lap. She's so beautiful it hurts to know she might never be mine.

CHAPTER 14

Jana

Barbara must be rubbing off on Kane. Instead of texting me, I get a message on the hotel line that says he'd like me to meet him up in his room for our weekly meeting at six thirty.

We're in Chicago, and although I didn't want to come—I've been dodging Kane for an entire week since I got drunk and made a fool of myself, handing him the opportunity to reject me—I have to attend this meeting.

Since I have no choice but to be there, I decide to dress *not* to impress. I stay in my workout clothes after I visited the gym downstairs, still reeking of sweat, but I throw a sweatshirt on over top. Instead of putting my gym shoes back on, I glide my feet into the pair of slides I usually wear around the hotel room. This way there's no possibility of Kane thinking my advancements were anything other than I drank too many damn seltzers. Of course, the shots didn't help either.

Leaving my room, I take the elevator to his floor and knock on the door.

He opens it, and the monster of an ache that's been living and breathing inside me since I called off our casual hookups roars to life. He's wearing gray sweatpants that hang low on his hips, a threadbare hockey T-shirt that he's probably owned forever, and he's barefoot. His eyes soak me up as much as mine do him. The tension we both ignore zaps to life like a power switch being turned to the on position.

"Come in." He steps aside and motions for me to enter his room.

He has a suite similar to mine. Bedroom and bathroom closed off, and a living space with a desk and television to entertain.

"I made the choices for dinner. I hope they're okay."

He walks over to the room service cart and lifts two silver domes to reveal a steak with a baked potato dish, and a chicken with rice and pasta dish. "If you'd rather have one to yourself, I'll take whichever you don't want. Or I figured we could share family style."

I sit down. "We can share. I'd never eat one of those meals by myself."

"You should try it sometime." Kane cuts the steak and potato in half.

"I don't have an eating disorder, if that's what you're suggesting?" I grab a fork and knife and cut the chicken.

"Not at all. I'm just saying I'd like to see you enjoy life a little."

I stop cutting and stare at him. "You think I don't enjoy my life?"

He never looks up from cutting the steak. I want to call him a chickenshit, but I refrain since we're trying to keep this working relationship intact.

"I think you have a lot of pressure on you. I think you find it hard to let loose. That's why it was so nice to watch you from the sidelines the other night."

Except he wasn't on the sidelines. His dick was in my hand, and he denied me.

"I was drunk. And just so you're aware, you aren't exactly a ball of sunshine yourself."

He gives me a wicked smile. "I know. I have a chip on my shoulder. I'm pissed off at a lot of things in this world when I should be thankful for the position I'm in. Do you know why you're not as happy as you could be?"

We end up splitting the plates and keep the pasta between us.

"I don't know." I reach for my water and take a sip.

"Bullshit."

I cut off a bite of steak and shove it in my mouth because it will take me longer to chew and give me an opportunity to think about how I want to answer his question. "Are you really asking me to throw years of therapy in your lap? I don't need fixing, Kane. I'm not looking for a relationship, especially marriage." I'm sure that's his angle.

He chuckles. "Who said I was?"

"Look at you. You're meant to be the patriarch of a family. The caregiver, protector, wearing a Father of the Year T-shirt. You take care of everyone, make everyone around you relaxed enough to be themselves because they know you can hold the weight of their problems."

He shakes his head and forks a piece of the vodka pasta. "Would it surprise you if I told you I don't want kids? Marriage, yes—if the right person comes along—but I don't want a family."

He's got to be kidding me. "Your brother—"

"Doesn't know shit. He wants me to have a family because he thinks that'll make up for our childhood. A do-over."

I don't want to pry, but I have a million questions I want to ask him. But if I ask him, I have to be okay with him asking me things. But maybe it's best we clear the air. Get all the reasons we shouldn't get involved out in the open. Talk about all the baggage we're both carrying through life. Perhaps that will make it easier to resist the man sitting across from me.

"What was your childhood like?" I ask, low and unassuming in case he shuts me down.

He looks up from his plate. "Are we really going to do this?"

Our eyes meet and I nod once. "I think so."

For a moment he says nothing, just holds my gaze. "My dad died in a work accident when I was really young, and my mom never picked up the pieces." He cuts into his chicken. "She fell into a depression, and though my aunt got her medicated, she rarely leaves the house. My aunt takes care of her now that Lee and I are gone, but growing up, it was me. I was the oldest, so..."

"You took over raising Lee, and that's why you don't want kids."

He shakes his head. "No. Raising Lee was hard when I was just a kid myself, but I don't want to bring a child into this world, into a family that's so unpredictable. My aunt always tells me my parents wouldn't have wanted this life for me. They would've wanted me to enjoy my childhood and not have to worry about making dinner, making sure the bills were paid and that my brother and I had clothes that fit us. I just decided at a really young age that I wouldn't have kids on the off chance they could end up in a similar situation."

Silence coats the room like a fresh coat of paint.

My heart aches when I picture a young Kane with so

much resting on his shoulders. But I know Kane doesn't want my pity, so I clear my throat. "That sucks, and I completely understand. It's funny how your youth can dictate your future, right?"

He nods. "Are you about to tell me why you're so uptight?"

I throw a piece of my roll at him. "I'm not uptight, but you're right that I rarely let loose." I shrug. "I told you about how my dad wanted a boy."

"I doubt that."

Dipping my head, I look at him from under my brows. "I didn't interrupt you."

He chuckles and holds up his hands in defense. "Carry on."

I lay my fork down beside my plate. "My dad taught me to hide my emotions from a young age. I remember when I was seven or eight, we were in a department store, and I wanted something. My mom said no for some reason. She rarely ever said no, and I threw a fit in the dressing room. My dad heard it, and when we got in the car afterward, he lectured me about how people were always watching us, judging us. Did I want to be the brat they assumed I was? And he was right. People were always paying attention to what I said and did because they knew who my dad was. The following Monday, a boy at school brought it up, and when I asked how he knew, he said it had traveled from some other person who saw it to his dad when he was at a party that weekend. I realized eyes *were* everywhere, and I didn't want my dad to have the bad press."

His large hand covers mine. "I liked your crazy side the other night. The carefree way you did what you wanted without thinking."

"Thank you for taking me out the back door."

"Anytime."

We continue to eat for a few minutes.

"Do you want a family?" he eventually asks.

I shake my head. "No."

"No kids?" He seems surprised.

I shake my head again. "And screw them up like you said? Mostly it's because I'm not cut out to be a mom. I'm not a nurturer. It's just not in my DNA." I shrug as though that doesn't bother me, but at the same time, I'm completely aware of the prick in my chest.

"I doubt that."

"If you saw me with a kid, you'd know. Ford and Lena's Annabelle cries every time I hold her. And when Paisley babysat when we were younger, the kids always complained about me being there. They'd say I wasn't fun. Once I worked at a camp because my dad said I had to learn the value of a dollar and a kid cut himself. I told him it was just a scratch and to continue playing."

He chuckles. "Maybe it was."

"He had to have two stitches after he complained to another counselor. I'm just not maternal, and I'm not going to invite something into my life that I'm going to fail at. Especially when it involves another person."

"So that's it then? You're scared to fail?"

I sip my water again. "Isn't everyone scared of failure?"

"I was for a long time, but you learn quick when you play a professional sport that you have to be okay with failure. It's inevitable. But it's still one of the hardest things to learn. I wouldn't have made it where I am without realizing I might fail, but I have to learn from it. The second time a situation presents itself, I should know better."

"So, fail the first kid but have a second one and I'm good."

We both laugh. It's a welcome sound after so much serious talk. When we finish our meal, I make my way to the couch while Kane rolls the cart back out into the hallway.

When he returns, he sits next to me. His thigh touches mine and he places his palm on my cheek. "I want to make something clear about the other night."

Our eyes meet, and my breath hitches in my throat. He's one gorgeous man.

"I didn't reciprocate that kiss, but not because I didn't want to. You have no idea how bad I did. You were drunk, and when I have you again, I want to know that you're not going to walk away from me." He lets his thumb drag back and forth across my cheek. "I know our time might not be right now, but there isn't anyone else I want to be with. That might not have been clear the other night, and I want to make sure we're on the same page."

"The same page being what?" My voice is low and heavy with lust because I want to crawl into his lap.

"Our time is coming, Jana. I know you want me, and it's okay if you're not ready yet. You just let me know when you are. I'm leaving the ball in your court. Come to me sober and open to seeing what this is between us, and you'll make me the happiest man on this planet."

My heart speeds up and I open my mouth, unsure of what to say.

"I kind of like you speechless," he says, his hand slipping off my skin, causing the small hairs on the back of my neck to stand. "Now let's talk shop."

He gets up and sits in the chair off to the side of the couch, giving me some space.

I thought this man hated me. I mean, I knew he was attracted to me physically, but I thought he loathed the person I am. How does he expect me to process this?

For the time being, I do what he says. I pull out my phone and open the notes app to make sure I go over everything we have to talk about.

Business first. Pleasure... later?

CHAPTER 15

Jana

"We get three days off and I have to spend them with you guys instead of my wife and my newborn." Warner falls back into one of the cushioned seats on the bus, looking dejected.

We just flew into North Carolina for the team-building weekend, which means no women except for me. From what Kane has told me, Warner hasn't been shy about his displeasure, acting like a teenager who has to go to his grandparents' for an entire summer.

The only empty seat on the bus is next to Kane, so I sit down, putting my purse on my lap. We haven't talked that much since he told me he's in when I am, but he seems fine with that and hasn't pressed the issue. It's not even that I'm avoiding him per se. I just don't know what to say. My head and my heart are at odds.

The bus starts with a stutter forward and I lurch forward for a second then back.

"Warner can't shut up," I whisper to Kane.

"I'll handle it." He glares over his shoulder at Warner, who has his head buried in his phone.

"It's not like we had a choice. Dad made us plan it."

"He's a grown man who gets paid millions of dollars to play for this team. He can suck it up for three days."

Some of the guys are in good spirits on the ride, making jokes about who will win what and letting their true competitive nature shine.

A half hour later, the bus pulls down a heavily wooded gravel road where a sign says, Adventure Quest—Where your employees start thinking as a "WE." It's a colorful sign with little words around the logo like vision, support, goal, plan.

After we've made our way down the long drive, the trees clear and the main building appears, surrounded by little cabins sprinkled through the area. A man and woman are waiting, waving ecstatically.

"They look like they haven't had human interaction in years. Where did you bring us?" Ford groans, grabbing his expensive leather carry-on from underneath the seat in front of him.

I widen my eyes at Ford. "Rumors have it that most Fortune 500 companies come here with their executives. Maybe even Jacobs Enterprises."

He laughs. "Not when my dad was CEO. He didn't believe in anything that took you away from the office."

"Until now." Warner chuckles. "You'd think the man had a lobotomy the way he coos with Annabelle and Jalen."

Ford smiles at his friend. "The other day he picked up Annabelle to take her to some art class only for grandpas. Be prepared."

They file out, and we wait for all the players to leave the bus.

"Are you ready for this?" Kane asks.

"Being the only female except for that woman out there? No. I feel like I should've brought Barbara with me." I stand and make my way down the aisle.

"Barbara needs a technology class, not a team-building retreat. And we're partners, remember?"

I glance over my shoulder.

He adds, "That was what we talked about at my house and—"

"I remember. I'd hate to be on Ford or Warner's team anyway. They're so ultracompetitive."

We step off the bus, and all the players are positioned on either side of the couple as though it's a receiving line. All their eyes are on us.

"Jana?" the woman says, her hands covering her mouth as though she's a long-lost relative I haven't seen since I was ten.

"Corin, right?" I walk down the gravel path, happy I dressed down on the plane. I put out my hand, but she shoos it away, thrusting herself into a hug with me.

"I'm Clark," a deep voice says next to me.

"Nice to meet you. Kane Burrows."

Finally, Corin lets me go and my mind is spinning before my eyes have the chance to land on Clark. Corin does the same introduction with Kane, except she smacks a kiss on his cheek, leaving red-lipstick residue.

"I cannot tell you how big of fans we are," Corin says.

"Of the Florida Fury?" I ask for clarification, because we're not exactly their local team.

"Hockey. Clark here watches it all the time. And we've dug deep in our treasure trove to find the best team-building skills for a hockey team." She glances around me at the players. "Oh my, you're all so... big." Her cheeks flush pink.

"Stop staring, Corin." He shakes his head at the woman I assume is his wife. "I'll show you to your cabins. Four to one, except for Coach Burrows and Miss Jana here. She gets to stay in the main house with Corin and me." Clark winks, and I step a little closer to Kane.

"Lucky you," he whispers.

"Yeah, lucky me." I smile brightly in case Corin or Clark overhear.

Clark leads the group, and the players split off into groups of four. No one bothers to argue. I'm surprised but impressed.

"Here's our smallest cabin, Coach Burrows. We know you can't be seen in your skivvies and be respected by your players. We usually use it as a time-out house when a team member can't behave themselves."

"Or they're too drunk," Corin adds. "But there's no alcohol on the premises." She points at the players with a warning glare a school nun might be jealous of.

"We've had people sneak it in. It's a little cramped, but I think you'll find it works." Clark opens the door, and all there is is one twin bed, small table, and a lamp.

"Thank you," Kane says graciously.

Warner pops his head out of the cabin next door. "Bathrooms? Showers?"

"Come with me." Clark waves him over. "It's all communal. Except Miss Jana gets to use the facilities in our house."

Corin winds her arm through mine. "I'm so excited. We rarely get women up here when we have a sports team on the grounds."

This is what I get for booking something last minute.

I smile tentatively at her. "Oh nice."

Kane coughs out a laugh.

Clark walks us over to a communal bathroom and outside showers.

"I'm going to freeze my nuts off," Tweetie says.

"I'll make sure the heater is on for the water," Clark says.

"And after we get out of the water?" Tweetie looks at everyone incredulously.

"It's only three days. Relax." Kane acts like the father of the group once again.

Clark claps his hands together. "For those of you not dressed in gym shoes and sweatpants and sweatshirts, go change. We'll be starting in a half hour."

The guys go scrambling, but Kane remains near me.

"You're with me, Miss Jana," Corin says and walks me toward the main house.

I stare back at Kane as though it's *The Hunger Games* and my name was just picked as tribute.

Corin shows me to a room that looks very farmhouse, but not the modern vibe you see in homes nowadays. There are white lace curtains I'm certain won't hide the rising sun, and the queen-size bed has two rows of pillows and a big lump in the middle.

"Clark and I are right next door. I apologize, but we'll all have to share a bathroom since our other one is on the fritz. But at least we're not outside with the boys, am I right?"

"Yes. Thank you very much." I wheel in my small suitcase, along with my laptop bag.

"What's in there?" Corin points at my business bag.

"Just my computer and stuff. I plan on working at night."

She reaches around me, and I assume she's going to admire the bag, maybe ask me where I got it, but she puts it over her shoulder. "No computers or phones." She holds out her hand. "Technology is the death of teamwork."

Where did the nice Corin go? The one who hugs you and makes you think she can't wait to have girl time?

"I don't think I read that on your website. We have some players with families."

She shoos me, and for a moment, I think she's going to

say she's kidding. "The company number goes to my cell phone. If someone calls with an emergency, I'll let whoever it is know right away and they can use their phone."

I crinkle my forehead and she thrusts her hand closer to me.

"Okay, I'm just going to shoot a text to my dad, so he knows I won't have my phone on me." I type out the message, being explicit about where I am. Then I pull up Kane's contact and send him a message.

Me: *They're going to take away our phones. Tell the players so they can text their loved ones now.*

Kane: *Clark already came around. Warner is currently on the ground holding his to his chest like a toddler with his toy.*

I power off my phone and hand it to her.

"Thank you. I hate it when people get protective about them."

I don't say anything because I'm pretty sure anything I said she wouldn't agree with anyway.

"Now get going. Clark doesn't like when people are late."

My head tilts. "I thought we had half an hour?"

She laughs. "If you wait until then, you're late."

Since I'm not about to find out what the punishment is if I'm late, I open my bag and take out a sweatshirt before walking downstairs. Once I'm out of the house, I find Ford wrestling with Warner for his phone. The rest of the team and Clark stare in a circle around them.

"Damn it. He bit me," Ford screams.

Clark looks at me, a bin full of cell phones hanging from his hand. "There's always one."

"He has a newborn," I say, coming to Warner's defense, though he needs to put a pin in it.

Clark just continues to stare at me.

"I think he's concerned his wife might need him."

Clark says nothing.

"Come on. My mom and dad are with Imogen and Jalen. They're fine," Ford says.

Warner gets the upper hand, but Tweetie jumps in, snatching the phone from Warner and holding it up and away from them.

"Here, Clark." Tweetie tosses it.

Clark fumbles trying to catch the phone and it drops to the dirt.

"Fuck, is it broken?" Warner shouts.

Clark looks at the phone in his hand. "No. It's all good. There's a main phone in our kitchen in case of any emergencies."

"Hell, who remembers anyone's numbers nowadays?" Ford says.

Warner scowls at me and heads back to his group.

"I'm going to take these to Corin. Back in a second." He points at Ford and Tweetie. "I see some star pupils already. The rest of you need to step it up."

The rest of the team look at one another like, What the hell did we do?

Once Clark isn't within earshot, Kane comes to my side. "How's your bedroom?"

"I get to share a bathroom with Clark and Corin."

He chuckles. "Lucky you."

"Maybe this was a bad idea? They took our cell phones." I cringe, and he laughs.

"I'll admit your dad usually planned something a little posher, with catered meals and an ample amount of alcohol.

I'm scared Clark is going to tell us we have to hunt for our food if we want to eat." Kane runs a hand through his hair.

For the millionth time today, I ogle him for a moment. My willpower is waning. I know it. Hell, he probably knows it. The fact that he doesn't want kids only pulls me to him more. At one point, I thought we couldn't be compatible because we wanted different things out of our lives, but what if that's not the case?

Kane said to come to him when I was ready, that he wouldn't rush me. But everyone has a breaking point, and I'm mindful that he won't wait forever for me.

Clark comes back out of the house. "Who's ready for our first team-building activity?"

The entire team groans.

"Enough. Make the most of this." Kane uses his authoritative voice. The same one I imagine he perfected when he was taking care of his younger brother.

I smile at him.

"What?" Kane looks at me, a small frown marring his face.

I shake my head. "Nothing."

"Blindfolds!" Clark says and tosses one to each group.

"Not how I'd like to use a blindfold," Kane murmurs next to me, his arm brushing mine.

I can't help but smile. Me neither.

Chapter 16

"Stay on task, Coach Burrows."
—Jana

Kane

I catch the blindfold Clark throws at us, a dozen ideas coming to mind about how I could use it other than whatever he has planned. Especially with Jana standing next to me. She hasn't said a word about us since that night in Chicago. I told her I'd give her the time she needs, and I will. She's worth it.

Clark puts together teams of four, and I end up with Jana, Tweetie, and Cory. Aiden, Ford, Maksim, and Warner are all on a team, which is completely unfair, but they're our starters and having them be a cohesive unit is important. The other teams are a mix of guys. Clark leads us to a large mud pit with a bunch of wood beams built across it.

"Suck it up. Let's go." Ford gives Warner his version of a pep talk.

I can't put myself in Warner's place, but I'm sure it sucks having to be away from his family. Still, he has a commitment to the team, and he needs to be here and participating.

"Okay, each team member has to get across the beam and back blindfolded while the person after them directs them through the exercise. First team to have all four members done wins. Now, strategize with your team and pick your order," Clark directs us.

"Let's get Jana across first," I say.

She shakes her head. "I'm not going first. I want to go toward the end."

Tweetie raises his hand. "I'll go first, but these are new sneakers, so do not let me end up in the mud."

"I'm pretty sure we're all gonna be in the mud at some point this weekend." I shake my head at him. "Okay, Tweetie, Cory, Jana, and I'll go last." I'm dictating, which isn't really how this should go, but now that I'm the coach, I'm having a hard time not being the decisive one in a group.

Ford's team is next to us, and they're all huddled and whispering.

"This isn't for the Cup, boys," Tweetie says.

Maksim flips him off with his hand that's on Aiden's back.

"Okay, enough planning. Let's go. Number one, put your blindfold on," Clark shouts to everyone.

Tweetie pulls his over his eyes, and Warner puts one on next to us.

"You can put your first foot on the beam," Clark informs them. "Ready and GO!"

It's hard to hear with everyone screaming, but immediately, two players at the far end are in the mud, swearing and yelling at their teammates.

"Tweet, just stay straight. Don't rush. Slow and steady," Jana says in a calming voice. "Move your right foot to the left a bit. That's it!"

"Warner, come on, man," Aiden says. "Move faster."

"It's really not about speed," Cory says to the group of four beside us.

Ford puts up his hand. "Mind your business, Jet."

"I'm just saying, he's already teetering," Cory continues.

I gotta hand it to the guy. He's talking trash, but he's doing it under the disguise of being helpful.

"Again, Jet, we got it!" Ford's flustered, and I inwardly chuckle.

Tweetie makes it back to us and hands the blindfold to Cory. Warner is only a few steps away.

"Let's remember my nickname." Cory winks at Maksim, who's getting ready to go once Warner is off the beam.

"Love the confidence, Cory," Jana says. "Now go."

Cory barely needs any guidance, as though he was a gymnast back in the day. It's amazing to watch him slowly but surely make his way across. Maksim is oddly balanced on his beam though and is making good headway.

Cory returns with a huge lead, jumping off the balance beam with the same sureness as he skates on the ice. Jana quickly puts on the blindfold, and way too many visuals spring to mind. I struggle to direct her at first.

"She's got no shot against Aiden," Ford razzes.

"I'm still your boss, Ford," Jana calls.

"You need to slow down, Jana," I shout. "You're going to go over."

"Then direct me," she says with that edge in her tone.

"Feel that breeze, Jana? That's Aiden passing you," Ford yells.

Jana flips him off, making her teeter a little before she regains her balance.

Ford eyes me. "Looks like it's me and you, Coach." He winks. I've never witnessed an ego as large as Ford's. Then again, that's what makes him the player he is. "Warner, get off your ass and direct me!"

Warner stands after sitting the whole time after his turn and watching the group wordlessly.

"You're here, now jump," I tell her.

Jana leaps instead of jumps, but she makes it. Then she's taking off the blindfold and putting it on me.

I lean down to whisper in her ear so no one will hear me. "Just so you know, I'm stealing this, and if you want to visit my little time-out cabin tonight, I'll have it with me."

"Stay on task, Coach Burrows." She smacks my ass to get me going.

"Ford's gone. You gotta go," Tweetie says.

The darkness takes a minute to get used to. I thought this would be easy, but fuck if I can't get one foot in front of the other.

"You're not really stepping. You're just sliding your feet!" Cory yells.

"I know what I'm doing."

God, this sucks. I'm an athletic guy. How can I not figure this out? I'm so busy ridiculing myself that one foot slips and I hold out my arms to steady myself.

"There you go. Get your balance back, Kane. You got this." Jana's voice stands out from the others, and I follow her directions. "You're at the end, don't go any farther. Now turn around slowly."

"There you go!" Cory shouts.

"Just like that." She's encouraging me to continue. "Ford's in trouble, so don't worry about him."

"Teamwork comes first," Clark shouts to everyone. "If you win without working as a cohesive team you're missing the point."

"Is there a trophy?" Ford asks.

"Well..." Clark hesitates.

"Then it's a race," Ford says.

From the sound of his voice, Ford is right next to me, so we still have a shot.

"Okay, you're almost back," Jana yells. "You guys are neck and neck. Can you go any faster? I'll tell you when to jump."

"It's too far away," Cory says.

"He's going to break his nuts," Tweetie says.

"He's fine. Don't wait until now to pipe up," Jana scolds them. "JUMP!"

I take two steps and jump, leaping with one foot in front of the other, but the tip of my shoe drags on the beam, and I end up in the mud pit.

"Only the last player off the beam can help a player in the mud," Clark calls.

"I'm coming!" Jana says. I reach out blindly to grab her hand, and eventually, her hand is on my forearm. "I'm not sure I'm strong enough for this."

"Why is this mud so fucking deep?" I say, trying to get some kind of grip. "Guide my hands to the beam. I'll push myself up."

"No, I can pull you. I'm lying on the beam."

"Just give up now. We won!" Ford says right before I hear his entire team roar in victory.

Jana is trying to get me up, but what happens is exactly what I figured would—she ends up in the mud with me.

"Ew!" she shouts. "It's so slimy."

"Okay, Cory, you can go help them now," Clark says. "You're fighting for second place."

Cory's already there before Clark can finish. "Let's go, you two." His hand finds mine and pulls. "Put your feet on the beam," he tells me, using his strength to get me up. "Tweetie, guide him to the end."

"Now, Jana, get on my back," Cory says, which has me oddly jealous for a split second.

By the time I get off the beam, we barely come in second and Jana and I are covered in mud. I'd say from her expression, she's ready to pack it up and call team building a failure right now.

"I'M SORRY, WHAT?" Jana asks Corin nicely, although her expression says she's about to rip out Corin's throat.

"No mud in the house. You'll have to shower with the boys. I'm sure they're willing to afford you some privacy." She hands Jana some clothes. "I took the liberty of getting some things out of your luggage for you." She leans in. "Your panties are very pretty."

Jana accepts the clothes with force, spinning away from her. "Thank you," she mutters and walks away.

"Oh wait," Corin says. I kind of hope for Jana's sake that Corin has changed her mind, but she just hands Jana a towel and a washcloth. "Here you go. Don't tell Clark though. Those are the good towels."

Jana and I look at one another for a beat.

"I'll get the guys out of the area and stand watch for you," I say.

She doesn't fight me on it. "I'm trying to be good with all this, but I have to say, I've never even been camping, Kane. I have no technology, no makeup... I don't feel like myself."

Most of the guys have already showered. They're throwing a football around the bonfire when we arrive at the showers.

"You're doing a great job, and no one can tell how out of your element you must be feeling," I say.

She looks up at me. "Are you in your element? Like Canada, is this what it's like?"

I smile at her and shrug. "I didn't shower outside."

She playfully pushes me. "I mean the outdoors."

"British Columbia is beautiful, so I spent a lot of time outside. I enjoy hiking and fishing. I think it's why I'm usually outside at my house when I can be."

"Who watches Rocky when you're gone?"

I'm oddly touched that she remembered my dog's name and she's concerned.

"Emma. She always starts by saying she'll let him out and take him for walks, but by the time I get home, he's usually at her house. She likes to complain about him being all up in Penny's grill, but she secretly likes it."

"It's easy for you to make friends, huh?"

I stop when we reach the showers. "I guess so. But I only have a few people I'd call true friends. Ones I'd call when I need help getting rid of a dead body." I chuckle. "Now go. I'll make sure no one bothers you."

"Thanks, Kane." She walks into the shower area.

I hear the water turn on and she screeches. "How did I get myself in this situation?" she says—more to herself than me, I think. "Just so you know, it's lukewarm at best."

"The guys probably used a lot of the hot water," I call.

"And Corin didn't give me my shampoo or conditioner, so now my hair is going to be all frizzy."

"No one here is judging you."

Ten minutes later, she comes out of the shower dressed in a pair of jeans and a sweater, her hair wrapped up in the towel. "Thanks for standing guard."

"You're beautiful." The words rush out of me like water from a crack in a dam. "I mean, without the makeup and the expensive clothes, you're gorgeous." She opens her mouth, but I put my finger to her lips. "I'm not suggesting you're not gorgeous with those things, but without them, you're just as stunning."

A small smile pushes her cheeks up and I let my finger drop.

"Thank you." Her voice is soft and serene, something you don't hear a lot of from Jana.

"I only speak the truth. If it's any consolation, you're doing an amazing job here."

She presses her lips together and steps closer. "Kane, I know you're waiting for an answer..."

I shake my head. "I meant it. Take your time."

"How would we navigate that? Technically I'm your boss. I don't want us to end up where we were before—when we hated one another."

"I never hated you, Jana. Not even for a second." My hand falls to her hip and the space between us shrinks to almost nothing.

"Me either," she whispers.

"I really want to kiss you," I admit, continuing to play my hand with the cards facing her so I don't scare her.

"I really want you to kiss me."

My heart thrums and I bend to reach her. Her tongue slides over her bottom lip and her hand moves to the back of my head. Finally, after months of not having her, I'm going to have a taste of her, even if it's only a small piece.

"*Shit!*" Warner crashes through the wooden partition separating the restroom from the open area next to us.

Jana pushes me away and rushes off.

I stare at Warner, who's lying on the ground surrounded by broken wood, clutching a football and all smiles. "I just needed a little competition to get my fire back. I'm all good now, Coach."

"You'll be paying for that." I eye the broken partition.

"No biggie." He stands and throws the football to Ford.

I watch Jana walk to the main house, and she stops right before she'll be out of view. Our eyes catch and she smiles.

Maybe this team-building thing isn't so bad after all.

CHAPTER 17

Jana

My mom taught me to always make sure I bring earplugs and an eye mask when traveling, and I'm thankful for her right now.

The bed is creaky and the blankets are heavy, but other than that, I had no complaints. Corin and Clark were polite about sharing the bathroom, and the more I'm around them, the less I worry that they're going to murder me in my sleep or steal my underwear as some weird sort of trophy.

But then the moans started, the light knocking of a headboard on our shared wall, and the vulgar words coming through the paper-thin walls. I hurry to put in my earplugs and bury myself under the blanket, praying I'm hearing animals outside.

"Oh, Clarky baby," Corin coos, which throws out my theory of two raccoons going at it on the roof.

I clutch the blanket tighter over me, pressing the foam things into my ears more, wishing I had music to play.

Eventually after they're done, I fall asleep. But now that it's morning, I'm having a hard time looking Corin in the eyes.

On my way out to the field with the guys, she stops me. "Miss Jana, I'm so sorry for last night."

I shoo her away, not wanting to discuss this topic.

"Clark isn't usually that spunky, so I had to take advantage of it. Woman to woman, I hope you understand."

I smile, unsure how to answer.

"But sorry if we kept you up, especially with all the hiking you'll do on the scavenger hunt today."

"I'm sorry?"

"I don't want you to be tired." She worries her bottom lip.

"No, you said something about a scavenger hunt and a hike?"

She waves off my concern. "Oh yes, just a few miles. No big deal."

"Great," I mumble and walk out the door.

"Just one text." Warner is bothering Clark when I reach the group. "He's a newborn."

"Clark, may I have a word?" I nod at him to join me closer to the showers just as Kane comes out of the bathroom looking delicious, running a towel over his still-damp hair. Clark follows me away from the guys, and it takes me a minute to move my attention back to him. "Listen, Warner's a new dad. Surely you understand how worried he might be."

"Do I go to the Florida Fury arena and tell you how to handle your team, Miss Jana?"

"Well..."

"Exactly. He gave his wife the number here. She will call if there's a problem and we'll get him to the airport should something arise. What do you think people did before cell phones?"

"That's the thing, Clark. We don't have to think about that because we have them now. These boys mostly grew up with them, so we can't expect them to just go cold turkey like that. They have young families."

He shakes his head. I swear he might be more stubborn than my dad. "I'm sorry, Miss Jana, my answer is no."

I nod and give Warner an "I tried" expression. He throws his orange juice container on the ground before grumbling and picking it up to throw it out.

Kane walks over to me. "No go?"

"Nope. How did everyone sleep?"

He shrugs. "They're all bitching. What about you?"

"You don't want to know," I say. "I might have to sneak into your room tonight."

"You're always welcome." He grins.

There's that spark again. The tension that's like a live wire between us.

"What's for breakfast anyway?" I look away from him at the folding tables that have been set out. The boys cannot complain about this. "Do you think Corin cooked all this?"

"Yes, she did," Clark answers, coming up to my side. "I got lucky when I caught her. She was up at four making fresh biscuits."

"They're incredible," Maksim mumbles over a mouthful. "Can I have my fiancée call you for the recipe?"

"Or you could bake them for Paisley?" I raise an eyebrow.

He points at me with the hand holding what's left of the biscuit. "I'd definitely get some action then. I love having her best friend here." He takes another one and two sausages before heading back to the fire that has chairs set up all around it.

"We're all going to smell like smoke on the plane," I grumble, picking up a piece of bacon.

"You better eat more than that. Clark told us this morning that it's a scavenger hunt in groups of two. I don't want to brag, but you scored the best partner." Kane winks and takes a plateful of eggs, sausage, and biscuits, then grabs another one for pancakes.

"Jeez, Kane." I stare at his plate in disbelief.

"Wondering where it all goes?" He lifts his sweatshirt with his free hand, showing off his chiseled abs. The same ones my fingers have traveled down more than a few times. My lips tingle, remembering when I explored his flat stomach with my mouth.

"Pull your sweatshirt down." I pick up a plate and put some eggs and bacon on it. I'm not really a sausage kind of gal, but I opt for one biscuit.

"Tempting, I know."

I stare at him for a second, then at the group of guys playing football again. "You're very flirtatious this morning."

"I think the wind is changing direction."

My head tilts. "What?"

"Nothing. Let's eat."

I follow him to the fire, and we position our plates on our laps. Kane puts his pancakes on the empty chair next to him.

"I'm exhausted." Cory sits down next to me. "No one told me Train is called Train because of his snoring. I thought it was because his body checks feel like a freight train hit you."

We laugh.

"Well, I had to hear Clark and Corin go at it for the majority of the night. Let's just say there's a very different side to them that they don't show us." I fork my egg and put a piece of bacon over it.

"Okay, you drew the shorter straw for sure. You can bunk with us. There's an extra bed."

"I can take that bed and you can have my little time-out room," Kane says quickly, and Cory chuckles.

"Thanks, Cory, I might take you up on that." I decide to

play this little game for reasons I don't understand. I guess Kane never struck me as the jealous type.

"Didn't you hear what he said about Train?" The line between Kane's eyebrows deepens.

"I have ear plugs. I'll be fine." I shrug.

Kane says my name in such a curt tone I can't help but laugh. Cory quickly joins me in laughing at him.

"Assholes," Kane mumbles.

IMMEDIATELY AFTER BREAKFAST, Clark gathers up the group while Corin cleans up all the dishes. I'd love to offer her a hand, but I'm stuck doing today's activity with Kane as my partner.

"You've got fifty acres to cover. You each have different paths and a different order and will cover the same amount of ground, so there's no cheating. When you reach each station, you're to take the envelope with your team number on it. It will tell you the next place to go. You have six stations in total to visit." Clark hands us each a map. "The landmarks labeled—the river, the bridge, the barn... you get the idea. First team to get back here wins."

Kane takes the map from my hands, and I keep our first clue.

"Easy," Ford says. He and Warner have their heads practically side by side, looking at the map.

"Remember this is about teamwork. You might only be able to rely on one person at times. Make sure you read each card carefully. The forest has eyes," Clark calls.

"Fuck." Aiden does a full-body shiver. "Someone tell Saige I love her, and she's not allowed to date after I'm gone." He makes the sign of the cross over his chest. I'm not even sure if he's religious or not.

"On the count of three, you can rip open your envelopes. One... two... three."

Each group of two blocks everyone else out as the envelopes are torn open.

Make a wish but don't take a drink.

WE SCAN THE MAP, trying to find anything that might fit that description. Kane points at the river, but the "make a wish" bit doesn't make sense.

"See you, suckers," Ford says, and he and Warner run into the woods.

"One of them probably won't come out," Kane mumbles.

I shake my head at them. "They're so competitive."

"I say we just let them win," Aiden says. "Maksim can have more biscuits and I'll work on my spiral." He tosses the football in the air.

"Everyone does it." Kane uses his stern tone.

Aiden grumbles.

Kane points at the water fountain on the map—all the way on the other side of the land. "I swear they did this on purpose."

We walk into the woods, following the map and trying to act nonchalant, but we must have the farthest to walk. At least no one else is around us right now. I've been craving some alone time with Kane because apparently, I'm an idiot who can't stop herself from developing feelings for him.

We're thirty feet in when he speaks. "I bet you never thought you'd be doing this?"

"I thought the worst would be that I'd get wet."

Kane uses his thumb to point at himself. "Well, worry not. This Canadian will protect you."

"Were you a hunter?"

He seems to find that idea amusing. "No."

"So, how are you going to protect me?"

"Are you questioning my manly instincts?" He jumps. "Shit. Did you see that?"

A little squirrel runs up a nearby tree and I side-eye Kane.

"It ran through my feet, okay?"

"I didn't say anything. Maybe you're a little more city than you like to think."

"Maybe. We need to go right here."

We take the path that veers right, and a half hour later, we finally arrive at the abandoned water fountain that sits in the middle of a small dry pond.

"Here's our next clue." I kneel to grab our envelope off the ground at the edge of the dried-up pond.

"We need to make a wish."

"There's no water and I have no change." I retrieve the envelope and stand.

"Just pretend. Eyes are everywhere. What if we're supposed to do it?"

As much as I hate it, Kane has a point. I close my eyes and wish for guidance on my decision with Kane. "Done."

"Did you wish you could be my girlfriend? Because you can, you know." He smiles at me.

"Oh my god." I bend over into a belly laugh. "You're really changing course, huh? What happened to the patient man?"

"I just wanted to be clear. Make sure you aren't getting any mixed signals."

I hold up my hands. "No mixed signals here. I'm clear on what you want."

"And it's not just to be in your pants. I want more than that." He keeps his intense gaze on me.

"Yep, I got you, Kane."

"Okay, let me see the envelope." He holds out his hand.

I pass it to him, looking out over the rolling landscape. "They have horses." I point at the neighbor's pasture in the distance. "I never had a horse."

"Daddy never bought you one?" Kane asks, pulling the piece of paper out of the envelope.

"Daddy?"

"I'm kidding. Sorry though, horses are out of my income level."

I turn to face him, my arms stretching on the wood-slotted fence that runs along one side of the pond. "Are you forgetting I know how much you make?"

He turns around the clue card, ignoring me. "'I'm a bed without sheets, and I'm always dirty.'"

I snatch it out of his hands. "Did you plan this?"

He holds up both hands and sits down to look at the map.

I sit in the grass alongside him and lean close to his face, smelling the soap from his shower. "What do you think, then?"

He moves his head, and our eyes catch, our mouths millimeters apart. "Jana?" His voice is rough, and I know what he's going to say.

"Yeah?"

"I'm giving you fair warning, if you don't want to be kissed, move."

I stay where I am. His one eyebrow quirks up, but I remain in place, swallowing all my fears and reservations because I know what saying yes to this kiss means.

"I warned you."

His lips smash to mine and my body stirs with the excitement of tasting him again. This time is different because it's more than just sex. He wants a relationship, and although I'm not sure how I'll handle that, these months without him have left me longing for what we had.

And not just the physical aspect. I miss his company and his presence in my life. Sometimes when he looks at me, I wonder what it would feel like to be his.

His arm glides up my spine, his fingers threading through the hair at the back of my head, deepening our kiss. My fingers gently touch his bearded cheek, unsure where to go. We've never kissed like this, with this much feeling. It was usually a quick kiss before a race to undress one another.

This kiss comes with expectations and promises. Surprisingly, I don't feel panic welling up inside me.

I'm lost in Kane when footsteps breaking branches echo through the forest.

"Over there!" someone yells.

Kane strips his lips off mine and stands. "Let's go. Flower bed is next."

He grabs my hand, pulling me up, then places a gentle kiss on my forehead. I know right then that being Kane's is going to feel pretty close to heaven.

CHAPTER 18

Kane

I need to be done with this team-building bullshit right now if I'm going to get Jana in my bed. She's there in wanting us to be together, I know she is, but we need longer than a few minutes alone.

I'm tugging her through the scavenger hunt, trying to get us to the end as soon as possible so we can relax and hopefully have a conversation about what she wants. We only have one more night here before we fly home.

We pass the other teams often, all of us going in a zigzag motion over the map it seems.

Jana and I are headed back to the starting point when we hear rustling in the woods behind us. Figuring it's another team, I turn to see who it is, but I see something furry instead.

"What is that?" Jana points at exactly what I see. A brown-haired animal in the brush that's coming at us fast.

"Come on." Not knowing what's headed our way, I pick her up and place her on a nearby tree branch that's only about five feet off the ground. I try to join her but lose my footing, falling to the ground.

"Kane!" she screams.

I'm on my back, surrounded by dead leaves and branches. I hate this fucking team-building shit.

"Oh." Her voice softens, then she laughs.

I move to get up, but my ankle is screaming in pain. Shit. I'm pretty sure I twisted it on the root of the tree.

The small brown thing emerges from a pile of leaves, only for us to see that it's a fucking dog. A Yorkie at that. What the fuck is a Yorkie doing in the middle of the woods?

Jana can't stop laughing as the Yorkie jumps on me, placing two paws on my chest to lick my face. "This is too funny."

I notice a collar on the dog and reach for it to pick up the dog and place it down beside me. It wags its tail and continues on its way.

"Do you think it's lost?" Jana asks with concern in her voice.

"Don't know. We can ask Clark and Corin about it when we get back. I've got bad news though." I cringe.

"What?" She jumps down from the tree. I'm not gonna lie, it's impressive.

"I think I twisted my ankle when the brown-haired monster was coming for us."

She bends down and lifts the end of my pant leg. Sure enough, my ankle is already swelling up and it's black and blue.

"One more and the trophy is ours!" Warner screams from somewhere in the forest, obviously in a better mood than before.

Once they're out of earshot, Jana looks at me. We've already got all our clues, which means we could win this thing. I don't think any other team would be as competitive as Ford and Warner, so they're probably our closest competition. The only reason we're done is because I pushed Jana for purely selfish reasons.

"Can you get up?" Jana asks.

"Maybe, but the finish line is still a long way away." I pull out the map to show her.

She bites the inside of her lip. It's not like if she was the one who was hurt; I could throw her on my back.

"I think we're done, Jana."

She gives me a scathing look. One I haven't been on the receiving end of for some time. She searches the area—looking for what, I have no idea.

"Would a walking stick help?" She hands me a long stick that wouldn't hold the Yorkie's weight, let alone mine.

"Honestly, it's fine. Just go ahead and tell them I'm here…"

She's not paying any attention to me though. It's like she thinks she's suddenly some outdoorsy Jedi Master who will be able to form a set of makeshift crutches out of sticks and leaves. It's oddly appealing watching her though. She runs off into the woods without another word, back the way we came.

I push up on my hands, using a log to sit on and investigate my ankle. I flinch when my hands touch the hot skin. Not a good sign. I move to stand, but it's too much. "Fucking hell."

A rattling noise comes from deep within the woods. A couple minutes later, Jana emerges with the rusty wheelbarrow we passed. It's marked on the map as a way for teams to know they're on the right path. So much for that.

"I'm not sure—"

"Burrows, you're getting in. Come on." She comes to my side and offers me her shoulder.

Her labored breathing makes her chest rise and fall, which gives me an excellent view since she stripped down to her sports bra half an hour ago. I try not to give her all my weight, but it's impossible.

"There you go." She leads me to the wheelbarrow, taking my hand and placing it on the tree trunk next to it. "I'm going to bring it to you. Let your butt fall into it."

She lowers it, and I gently sit.

"Perfect. This is perfect." She's so happy. Who am I to burst her bubble and mention that she still has to push me out of the woods? She peers over the handles and looks upside down when I look up at her. "Okay, ready?"

"Yeah." I can't help the amusement in my tone because there's no way she's ever going to be able to move me, wheelbarrow or not.

"You can doubt all you want, but we've gotten this far."

She pushes and we go nowhere.

"I think I'm too heavy."

"I work out, you know. I might not look like it, but I do kickboxing and cycling. I have muscles."

"No one said you didn't. It's just that I'm about twice your weight."

She grunts, pushing the wheelbarrow until she grunts again when we don't move.

"Let's just think of something else."

Her eyes narrow on me. "No. One more time. Once I get it going, it won't be that hard."

I use the tree to push off with my arm while she pulls up and pushes on the handlebars, exhaling loudly. We move an inch and I almost topple over, but she steadies me, walking slowly to get used to the weight she's carrying.

"You did it!" I honestly can't believe it. I'm impressed.

"Don't sound so surprised." She huffs and puffs as we go faster.

"I'm so proud of you."

"Thanks, I guess."

She's probably taking that as an insult, but not a lot of

women I know would go to all this effort to win. It's hot as hell that she took charge of this shitty circumstance.

She's sweating by the time we see Clark and Corin in the clearing. We hear footsteps behind us, and we both look to find Ford and Warner not far behind.

"Hold on, Kane!"

Jana goes into a full sprint, the wheelbarrow teetering and tottering left to right. I swear my balls tuck themselves up into my body because I just know I'm going to go down hard.

"Shit! No way you're ahead of us!" Warner shouts, and Jana pushes herself harder.

I forgot about the small hill, and I think Jana did too. We're moving faster and faster until she loses her grip and I'm tumbling out of the wheelbarrow. I roll a couple of times, careful to keep my foot raised so I don't injure it further.

"Oh crap! I'm sorry." Jana looks down at me, then back behind us.

"You're not there yet!" Ford screams.

Jana grabs my arm and I use my good leg to sort of crab crawl on my back.

"Hurry!" Jana screams.

I move faster, hitting the finish line right before Ford and Warner cross seconds after us.

"She helped him. That's a disqualification!" Ford points at us.

Jana's on the ground and my head is on her stomach, both of us struggling for breath.

"Kickboxing was not good preparation for this, just for the record," she mumbles.

Ford and Warner are still arguing the authenticity of our

win with Clark, and he says, "It's called teamwork, guys. Her teammate was injured, and she was quick on her feet to get the wheelbarrow. Then when that failed, they worked together to reach the finish line." Clark looks at us. "They're the winners."

"Bullshit!" Warner yells.

"Don't be a sore loser," I say, sitting up. "But I do need someone to look at my ankle."

"Maybe Dr. Marc the Podiatrist is around," Warner jokes, and Ford gives him a disgruntled look.

"No Dr. Marc, but I'll call Dr. Isaac." Corin heads off to the main house.

When I catch Jana's eye, I mouth thank you, meaning it all the way to my core. She shakes her head like it was nothing, but it wasn't nothing to me. In fact, I think I just fell for her a little more.

DR. ISAAC ARRIVES and looks at my ankle, telling me it's a bad sprain. He wraps it and gives me a set of crutches to use until I get back to Florida to see my regular doctor.

We're at the bonfire after dinner. Tomorrow we have some sharing session in the morning, then we get back on the bus to drive to the airport to fly home. My bed sounds so good right about now.

Corin stands and claps. "Okay, it's ten o'clock, which means bedtime!"

Jana stands up next to me, and I clasp her hand for just one more touch. Her smile is illuminated by the flames.

"Come on, we'll help you get to bed." Ford and Aiden come over and offer me each a shoulder to balance my weight. The crutches aren't worth shit with all the uneven ground.

"I think he should be allowed to stay in the main house," Jana broaches the subject with Corin one more time.

"I'm sorry, but as I said, Clark doesn't allow any other men in the house."

"But Kane is injured. Surely, he can see this circumstance is different."

"It's okay, Jana," I say, appreciating the effort.

"See? He's fine. Now you come, Miss Jana. Bedtime."

I head to my small cabin with the help of the guys, and Jana heads to the main house with Corin. I'm not gonna lie, I'd hoped that they'd let me stay in Jana's room. Not that I would've had sex with her in someone else's house, but just to be near her. Thank her again for doing what she did for me.

"Thanks, guys," I say when they deposit me on my bed.

"No problem." Ford runs his hand through his hair. "She really went the distance to make sure you guys won. Reminds me of Lena."

"Yeah. Don't be too jealous of our trophy." I nod toward the generic gold trophy with two people holding hands on top.

"I might steal it, so be careful," Aiden says. "Who knew Jana had that in her?"

We all agree. They leave, and I lie in my bed, going over all the events of today. Rehashing and dissecting every look Jana gave me, everything she said. From our kiss at the water fountain to running from station to station, to her eyes lighting up when she showed up with the wheelbarrow. When we first met, I never thought she had this many layers. I'm ashamed to admit that I assumed things about her because of her family name, and she continues to prove me wrong.

My eyes slide closed for a moment, fatigue from a full day of being outdoors taking over, when my door creaks open.

I sit up, hoping this isn't Warner about to cry to me about missing his family. And I really hope it isn't Corin or Clark. I could see them having some agreement about sex with other people.

"Hey," Jana's sweet voice whispers.

"What are you doing here?" I whisper back.

"I want to be here with you, plus they're at it again." She touches the side of the bed and I slide over to the wall, giving her room to slide in. "Do you mind?"

"Are you crazy? Come here."

She climbs under the sheet, and I wrap my arm around her waist, tucking her into my side. "Are you sure this is okay? I've never gone to a boy's room before."

I laugh and she pinches my arm, sobering me up because no one can know she's here.

"I'm not a boy, Jana."

"I know that. I just meant..." She turns to face me, and her hands locate the sides of my face in the dark. "This is me making the move."

"Meaning?"

"Meaning, let's give this a try. You and me."

Relief rushes through me, and for a moment, I feel euphoric. Even the throbbing pain in my ankle is a distant memory. I bend forward to kiss her, and she presses her finger to my lips.

"But let's just keep it between us."

"Until the end of the season. After that, we go public."

She leans her forehead on mine. "If we're still together. Deal."

"Oh, we'll still be together." I lower her to her back and bring myself on top of her, which is a little harder to do with only one leg. The pain will be worth it. "That I can promise."

I seal that promise with a kiss I hope she never forgets.

CHAPTER 19

Jana

I was nervous before stepping into Kane's small cabin. What if he didn't want me to bother him right now? He has a sprained ankle, and I'm sure he's tired, but I couldn't listen to Corin call Clark daddy anymore.

Kane's balancing his weight over me, and I reach for his face in the dark, his beard scratchy against my palms.

"Me on top," I whisper. "You're hurt."

He allows me to flip him onto his back, a sure sign that he's in more pain than he's letting on. His hands grasp my waist, his thumbs running over my hip bones. Trying to take control, he runs my center over his erection. I sigh and place my hands on his chest.

I always kept it to myself when we were hooking up, but I've never had a lover who read my body the way Kane does. But that speaks to the man he is in general. Of course it would transfer to the bedroom. He's consistently doing for others, putting their needs before his own.

One of his hands travels up my side, and goose bumps chase his fingers. He grasps the back of my head and urges me down until his lips meet mine. The kiss starts slow and exploratory, but the more I grind along his length, the firmer the press of his lips, his tongue becomes more demanding, and our rhythm more frantic. One of the things I love about Kane is that he's not timid. He's sure of his skills and it's sexy as hell.

"God, I feel like I'm in a dream. Tell me I'm not," he whispers. "I'm not hallucinating, right?"

I giggle, low enough that hopefully no one hears us. "I'm right here in the flesh."

His hand on my hip tightens as if he has to check himself. "I finally wore you down, huh?"

"Yeah. I can be stubborn."

"I knew you'd come around. I mean, I'm Kane Burrows."

I lightly slap his bare chest, and he grabs my hand, tugging me down so I'm completely flat over him. He turns my head to kiss my jaw, and his tongue travels the length and down my neck.

"Too many clothes," he murmurs against my skin. His hands glide under the bottom of my pajama shorts, palming my ass. "And you're cold as fuck."

"I figured you'd warm me up."

He kisses my earlobe before nibbling. "Anytime, baby. I'll warm you up anytime."

Shivers rack my spine. His hands travel down to the sides of my shirt, grab the hem, and pull the fabric over my head, leaving me bare from the waist up.

"They missed me, right?" He palms my breasts, his thumbs and forefingers pinching my nipples. My body stiffens as the sensation travels down between my legs.

"Yeah."

"I knew it." He urges me up slightly until my breasts are right in front of his face. "I missed you two. Don't worry, I won't let her take you guys away from me again."

"Are you seriously talking to my breasts?"

"This is an *A* and *B* conversation, baby."

"Then I'll take my *C*s somewhere else." I move to sit up, and he presses his hand to my back, yanking me back down.

When I open my mouth for another retort, he brings one breast to his mouth and his tongue plays with my nipple. I arch my back and bend forward, giving him my entire breast. From the first time we slept together, he figured out that I love my breasts being played with.

He moves to my other breast, his mouth hot on my bare skin. I moan, and he takes his mouth off my breast to shh me, then uses just the tip of his tongue to circle my nipple in a teasing motion.

I want to scream his name, make sounds that tell him to continue what he's doing. I've never had sex when we have to be quiet, and I can't even see him enough to see what he's thinking. I slide down his body, even though he tries to get me to stop with his hands under my arms.

"You have too many clothes on." I hook my fingers into his pants and boxer briefs and drag them down his legs, careful about his ankle.

I can just make out his dick in the dark room. God, he really is a gorgeous creature. I have no idea how I've been able to exist with him these past few months.

"Tell me you're still on the pill." His voice sounds desperate.

"Tell me you've been tested?"

"I haven't been with anyone since you, but you probably have my test results from the team. I'm clean."

I smile, happy he can't see me in the dark. I don't want him to know how happy it makes me that he hasn't slept with anyone after me. "Me too."

"There hasn't been anyone else?" His hand gingerly

touches my cheek, his thumb brushing back and forth in a soothing manner.

"No." I shake my head.

"And the pill?"

"Still on it."

"And you're okay not using a condom?"

I stand off the bed, hook my fingers into the sides of my silk pajama shorts, and push them down my legs. "Is this answer enough for you?"

His hand molds and squeezes my ass until I climb back on top of him. "Ride me, baby. Just like you used to."

I straddle his waist, and he runs his fingers through my wetness, making sure I'm ready for him. He rubs small circles on my clit and a noise gets stuck in my throat.

Yes, I need more of that. God, I've missed this man. Impatient to feel him fill me after so long, I position myself over him and sink down on his length.

I hear him sucking on his fingers. "Still taste so fucking good."

His words get me going, and I move up and down and back and forth, my hands anchoring on his hard chest. He plays with my breasts as I circle my hips.

"You know I can handle more," he whispers, inching up on his forearms and making kissing noises to signal that he wants me to kiss him in the dark.

I bend and kiss him, his fingers surprising me when they pinch my nipples and I'm lost in his lips. I circle my hips, rising up and back down on his length. He whispers how beautiful I am, how soft my skin is, how great I feel wrapped around him.

In the dark, I forget all the reasons why we shouldn't be together. Why I don't want a relationship. Because to spend every night like this for the rest of life sounds like a pretty fantastic life.

The wall I built around myself is slowly leveled as Kane moves in and out of my body and whispers words of promise and praise. For once in my life, the guy wants me for me and not for who I am.

"You were so hot today. The way you took care of that situation? It turned me on so much."

I end up completely on top of him, my breasts smashed to his strong chest, and he hammers his hips up and down from below. I stifle my cry by pushing my face into his neck.

He seems to grow frustrated with this position and switches me onto my side, lifting one of my legs up and over his. He thrusts inside me slow and steady, his hands on my breasts and his mouth on my neck. The drag of him in and out of me is the most delicious friction, and I feel my orgasm getting close.

"I've never felt this way about anyone, Jana. I want you to know that. It's like you're my reward for waiting my entire career to find someone."

I move my hand to cover the back of his head, turning to kiss him as much as I can in this position. I hope my actions say everything I want him to know. All the words and promises I want to give him get lost when his fingers trace down my belly to my clit. He applies just the right pressure, as if my preferences are like riding a bike and he'll never unlearn them.

It doesn't take long until my orgasm crests and I clench harder, making him groan in my ear. I fight it off, but he continues to drill inside me, his fingers playing my clit like the master he is.

"I'm gonna come," I whisper.

"I'm here."

And I know he means so much more than catching me when the exhaustion of coming so hard hits me, but I lose the fight and stars light up behind my eyelids. His hand comes up and directs my chin to face him, his lips covering mine. As I ride the waves of the orgasm, his tongue plays magic in my mouth, and he swallows my cries.

He thrusts a few more times before stilling inside me and groaning into the hair at the back of my head. We both collapse on the bed, my head on his arm.

He kisses my temple and draws out of me. "Grab my T-shirt. It's on top of my suitcase."

I reach over and he takes it from my hands, cleaning me up. Taking care of me like he always does.

We snuggle into each other, face to face, and he kisses my forehead. "Get some sleep."

"I'm not tired."

"You need your sleep because when we get home, you're coming to my house, and I don't plan on us sleeping all night."

I smile as he tucks me under his chin, his arms wrapped around me as though I'm his favorite blanket.

I'm not sure how long we're asleep before a scream echoes through the night.

We both startle awake.

"Oh my god, they found out I left." I cannot believe I'm scared of Clark and Corin. I'm a grown woman who can sleep with whoever I want, whenever I want.

"I don't think so. It was way too close." His voice is rough and sleep-logged.

"Fuck!" another deep voice whisper-screams outside. "Go away."

Kane rolls over me and sits up, putting his sweatpants on carefully, then hops up on one foot.

"I'll go."

He glances back, grabbing the crutches. "You're insane if you think I'm letting you out there first."

"At least I'm not hurt."

"Jana, not now."

"Don't treat me like I'm some damsel in distress. Let's remember who got you to the finish line today." I grab his blanket and wrap it around myself, walking over to him.

"I know, I know. You're a badass. But right now, I'm not letting my... I'm not letting you go out there in the woods without me." He opens the door and the smell of a skunk leaks into the cabin.

"*Ugh*." I cough and almost throw up.

"It's just a skunk," Kane says. "Aren't you glad I didn't let you go out there now?"

I smile. "Yes. Thank you."

I rise to my tiptoes and kiss him. He wraps his arms around my waist, pulling me flush against him while still balancing on one foot. Impressive.

"I thought you wanted sleep?" I tease.

"Did I say that? Funny, I don't remember saying that."

"Coach," someone whispers from the other side of the door. "Hey, Coach?"

There's literally nowhere for me to hide, so Kane only opens the door a sliver. "Ford? What the hell?"

"It's Warner. He got skunked."

"You've got to be shitting me." Kane lets the door go to run his hand through his hair, and it opens enough to reveal me to Ford.

Ford's eyes widen enough that it's obvious, even in the dark. "Damn. Sorry for interrupting."

"This is none of your business." Kane shuts the door in Ford's face.

"So much for keeping it between us," I say, shaking my head.

Last time, we kept us sleeping together quiet for over a year, and this time, we only last one night. Go team.

But I find I care less than I probably should. I need to figure out why that is.

CHAPTER 20

Kane

"*Y*ou have to go help," Jana says.

"The dumbass was probably trying to get to his phone."

"Still. You're the coach."

I roll my eyes and open the door to Ford's shit-eating grin. "Nailing the boss, huh?"

I put up my hand. "I suggest you stop right there."

He shrugs. "Just an observation."

Using my crutches, I stumble after Ford until we reach the firepit. Warner, Tweetie, and Cory are already there.

After I scowl at the stench, I plug my nose. "Goddamnit, Langley, what were you doing?"

"I think we have to pee on him, right?" Tweetie says.

"No, you idiot, we need tomato soup," Cory corrects him.

"I swear it's pee on him. I'm happy to help you out." He starts lowering his pajama pants.

"That's jellyfish sting, you asshole." Warner runs in the other direction, causing the waft of the skunk stench to float over to the rest of us.

"Stop moving!" I yell, then we all look toward the house.

When no lights turn on, we huddle together again.

"What were you doing?" I ask again, because I'm sure I know why Warner was skulking around this time of night.

"I didn't think they lock the doors," he says all innocent, like a schoolboy who just tripped another boy at recess.

"Your phone?" I ask, and Warner nods.

"Imogen—"

"Is fucking fine. She can survive without you for three days. Good to know you can't survive without her. She'll be happy to hear that."

My cabin door opens, and all eyes turn to see Jana walking out, wrapped in a blanket.

Most of the guys snicker quietly, a "way to go, Coach" thrown in there.

"Why are we all standing around? Is no one fixing the problem?" She plugs her nose.

"There was a debate—" Tweetie starts, but Cory's quick to intervene.

"No debate," he says.

"Someone has to sneak in the house and see if they have tomato soup," Jana says.

"You're the only one allowed in the house," Ford says. "The rest of us? Clark might be a gun enthusiast or some-thing." He touches the tip of his nose with his finger.

Warner quickly does it also. Soon every one of them has their finger on their nose, including Jana, by the time I catch what's going on.

"We're not grade schoolers," I say.

"No, but you lost, so you have to go in," Ford says.

For a moment, I stare at Jana in disbelief.

"I don't want to be caught going through their stuff. Who knows what kind of punishment Clark might have in mind for something like that. You wouldn't want to put me in a situation that makes me uncomfortable, would you?" She gives me the most innocent expression I've ever seen on her face.

"I'm on crutches," I argue.

No one says a thing.

I shake my head at Jana. "While I'm doing this, you better figure out where you're going to put him to soak in it!" I point at each of them and dramatically put my finger on the tip of my nose. "Not it."

I don't wait around for them all to join in. I go in through the back door. Warner's suspicions were right—they don't lock their doors. Luckily, the kitchen is right there, so I use my crutches to head to what I think is the pantry. It's as if Corin knew I was coming; she has those cloth grocery bags hanging on the inside of the door. I take one and find two cans of tomato soup, which isn't nearly enough to cover Warner's body.

"What's going on in here?" The light turns on, and I squint for a moment. Clark is standing there in tight white briefs, his belly protruding over the waistband.

"Sorry, Clark, one of the players got skunked. We were trying to handle it ourselves."

"*Corin!*" Clark shouts.

"Honestly, we can handle it. Just... do you have any more soup?"

Clark laughs. "No, no. Corin has a special remedy. Bring him into the house and she'll take care of him."

"How so?" I ask.

"She'll bathe him with her homemade concoction."

"Oh."

"Well go, it's the middle of the night."

Going as fast as I can on my crutches, I head back to the cabins.

"We saw a light go on. Who woke up?" Jana asks.

"Right now, they're both up. And they want Warner to come up to the house."

"Hell to the no," Warner says. "I'll just go home like this."

"No way!" we all yell.

"Come on. I guess Corin has some magic recipe or something." I use one of my crutches to point toward the house.

Warner tentatively stands while his head hangs low. "Fuck. Fuck. Fuck."

I don't say a word about Clark mentioning Corin bathing Warner. What happens in that house is between them.

I go to pat Warner on the back but pull back at the last second. The last thing I need is to be on crutches and smell like a skunk. "Good luck."

"You're not coming with me?"

"No." I laugh.

We all watch him go in the back door.

"Way to keep it old school, Clark," Warner says loudly enough for us to overhear.

Everyone else looks confused, but I know he must be referring to Clark's tighty-whities.

The bathroom light turns on upstairs and we all watch from below as though a movie is about to play out.

"Shit, I'm glad I'm not him," Ford says. "What do you think they're doing?"

"Trying to get him to join a threesome?" Tweetie asks.

"Stop it. They're fine people. Odd, but fine," Jana chimes in.

The smell must be overwhelming inside because the windows start opening, which allows us to hear more of the conversation. Corin opens the bathroom window, and we see a silhouette of Warner.

"Oh, I can do that, ma'am. No need. My wife wouldn't like it if you touched me there."

Ford bends over in a fit of laughter.

Aiden sits on a chair on the back patio and props his feet up on the chair next to him.

Maksim says he's going back to bed.

Tweetie winces. "Awkward."

"It's just a mixture. I'll run this over your skin with a washcloth, let it sit for five minutes, rinse, then do it again," Corin says.

The water turns on and drowns out all conversation after that.

We all decide to stay until Warner emerges from the house. An hour or so later, he passes by us and goes right to his cabin.

"Whoa, whoa, what happened?" Ford asks.

"I don't ever want to talk about it." Warner disappears inside and we all crack up.

"At least you don't smell like skunk. Imogen will be happy for that."

"Shut up, Ford," Warner mumbles from inside.

Tweetie laughs hysterically, Ford follows Warner inside, and everyone goes to their cabins.

Once all eyes are out of view, I drop one of my crutches and take Jana in my arms. She wraps the blanket around my body, and we stare at the stars.

"It is beautiful here," she whispers.

"You're beautiful," I say back.

"Gross! Go to bed!"

"Ew!"

"Mom and Dad, stop!"

I shake my head, and Jana kisses my jaw. "Let's go to bed."

"Happily."

THE NEXT MORNING, we come out of the cabin as Corin is setting a plate of pancakes on the table.

"I had a feeling," she says to us.

Jana's wearing my Fury sweatshirt since she only had silk pajamas on, and damn if it doesn't look perfect on her.

"I mean, all that ruckus and you never woke up?" Corin says.

"I'm sorry." She looks back at me and smiles, and I know she's not sorry at all.

After Warner's bath last night, we went back to my cabin and I feasted on Jana's pussy until she came apart on my tongue. No chance she's sorry about that.

"We've kind of been on and off—"

"Oh, you don't have to explain anything to me." Corin leans closer. "If Clark looked like that..."

I puff my chest out a bit. Jana rolls her eyes at me then heads to the main house to get dressed and packed.

When she wheels her suitcase to join the rest of us where the bus will arrive, I give her a chaste kiss.

Clark and Corin join us.

"Thank you," Jana tells them. "This was great for our team."

"I know it's not fancy, but I think something good happened this weekend," Clark says.

"Not sure Warner feels the same," I say.

Everyone laughs.

Clark hands Jana the bucket of phones, and I pass them out to everyone. They're like teenagers, booting up their phones in a frenzy after being grounded from them. They all disperse in different directions, returning phone calls.

Warner FaceTimes Imogen. "It's been hell, Gen, you have no idea what I've been through."

"My time hasn't been all rosy here either. Hurry home." Her voice lowers. "My father is driving me crazy."

The bus drives up the gravel lane, and we all say our goodbyes to Corin and Clark. Jana and I sit next to one another on the bus, and I put my hand over hers as though it's normal. Our normal. And it feels so right.

"Come over to my house tonight?" I ask her.

"Okay." I'm pleased that she doesn't have to give her answer any thought.

"Great, I'll make you a dinner and it won't be pizza this time."

"What can I bring?"

"Just yourself."

She rests her head on my shoulder and her eyes slowly close, the entire weekend catching up with her.

CHAPTER 21

"I thought I just did that."

Kane

A few weeks pass and I'm honestly shocked to find that the Fury are sitting at number one in our division. Which is awesome since I'm a first-year coach, although I was handed a pretty stellar roster. Even without the Fury though, I'd be happy as hell because something at that team retreat triggered Jana to open up and let me in.

We've been on a four-day stint of away games, and although Jana would normally join us, she had some meetings at home that she couldn't miss and couldn't reschedule, so I'm in desperate need of a Jana fix. I open the door of my place, ready to drop my bags and go get Rocky from Emma's, but Rocky runs to me the minute the door opens.

"Emma?" I call, assuming she's here and was nice enough to bring Rocky to me.

I bend down and drop my bag before petting Rocky behind the ears the way he loves. He falls to the ground on his back and his left foot moves as if he's trying to ride a bike.

"Sorry, no Emma." Jana leans her shoulder on the wall, looking casual with bare feet and wearing a pair of jeans and a sweater that hangs off one shoulder. Damn, she's so sexy. "I hope you're not disappointed."

The smile on her face says she already knows my

answer. And the fact she somehow got into my place and picked up my dog that she wasn't so crazy about at first says how far this woman has come in the past few weeks.

"Well, I did want to hear about her new painting..." I leave Rocky panting and whining for more attention and head right to my... well, we haven't discussed titles yet, but I'd say she's my girlfriend. I wrap my arm around her waist and tug her so she falls forward, bracing herself with her hands on my chest. "This is a great surprise."

"Wait until you try what I made for you. That might be the bigger surprise—just how awful a meal can be."

"I get you *and* dinner?" I kiss her softly. "Show me."

I follow close behind her, unable to take my hands off her as we head into the kitchen.

"My parents' chef gave me the recipe and said it was supposed to be easy, but I think she overestimated my abilities."

The chicken and rice on my plate looks hard in appearance alone. The only thing that appears somewhat edible is the salad. I sit on the breakfast barstool and pick up a fork, piercing a piece of chicken. It's a little burned and very dry, making it a struggle to swallow.

"It's terrible!" Her shoulders fall.

"No. Not terrible."

She points at me. "I can tell from your face."

I fork another piece and put some rice with it. "If it was terrible, would I take more?"

She leans over the counter and her sweater dips, giving me a glimpse of her bra-covered breasts. Now I'm hungry for something besides food. "You would just to make me feel better."

I set down the fork and open my arms and legs for her to cuddle into me. She takes the nonverbal command and comes around the island to me. I position her on my lap. "Honestly?"

She nods.

"It's not great."

She sulks.

"But I messed up a dinner too. Remember taco night?"

Her forehead falls to my shoulder. "I guess you'll have to deal with a... person in your life who knows she can't cook so she just orders takeout every night. Personally, I find it much easier anyway." She leaves my lap and opens the oven to show me foiled-covered containers she obviously ordered as backup.

"How much longer?" I ask.

"It's just warming. We can eat whenever."

"Good. Come here."

She knows what I'm thinking because her eyes light up as she walks toward me. Once I secure her with her back to the counter, I grip her hips and hoist her up, rising from the chair. Thank goodness my ankle is much better. I can't skate yet, but I can put pressure on it now. Since she's been riding me a lot during my rehab, it's time I pay her back.

"You just called yourself a person in my life." I squeeze her sides and she giggles, her hands wrapping around me, her long nails scraping the back of my neck. "What exactly does that mean?"

"I don't know. Are we a label type of couple?"

My hands rest on the hem of her sweater, teasing her as I run my fingers under the soft fabric. "I'd like to call you my girlfriend," I say, knowing this could cause a fight, or worse, cause her to run.

"Really?"

"And in turn, I'm your boyfriend?"

She rests her head on my shoulder and I wrap my arms

around her torso, running my hands up her back. She arches into me and slides closer to the edge of the counter as if she can't get close enough to me. It's one of my favorite things she does. Like an affectionate cat snuggling up to her owner.

"Okay," she whispers.

My heart bursts that she made it that easy. She held me at arm's length for so long, the last few weeks I've been shocked by how much she's taken to our new situation. There's only one thing we still have to navigate. "If I'm your boyfriend, I think we need to tell your dad."

She draws back and shakes her head. "I'm not ready for that."

"The team knows, Jana." I cradle her face, my thumb running over her plump bottom lip, which I love to nibble. "It's only a matter of time before someone spills the news by accident."

The fact we've gotten this far is amazing.

She seems to think about it for a moment, then she nods. "I'll plan a dinner."

"Good." I pick her up and she straddles my waist. "Now, dinner can wait. It's been a long four days."

I take her to my bedroom, which isn't much except for the French doors at the far end that open to the Gulf. I place her on my bed, but she shakes her head and falls to her knees in front of me. She looks up at me with those eyes that still hold a little hesitation, as if she hasn't given herself fully to me, but I know in time she will.

She unbuttons and unzips my pants, and they fall to my ankles. Rubbing my hard length with her palm over my boxer briefs, her fingers wrap around the waistband, and she drags them down, securing them under my swollen balls. My dick bobs out and shoots north. Her pink tongue slips out of her mouth, running along her bottom lip, and she takes the base in her palm.

"Goddamn, you're beautiful." Not just because she's on her knees, or the fact she's about to spread her lips and slide my cock into her hot, waiting mouth. It's her, the way she looks, the way she feels, the person she is that I can't get enough of.

She smiles up at me, guiding my dick into her mouth, then my eyes close from the rush of pleasure shooting through my cock directly to my balls. I manage to control myself, not shooting into her mouth right away. Instead, I enjoy the view. Her head bobbing, her tongue licking, the pumping of her fist. I reach for the back of her neck—not to guide her, she's perfect. I just need to touch her. My fingers grip her hair when she deep throats me and releases me slowly before doing it all over again.

"I'm barely hanging on," I tell her, and she increases the speed, her moans getting the best of me. Then she uses her free hand to unbutton her jeans and her hand disappears under the waistband. "Wait for me. I'll get you off."

She squeezes my balls with one hand, then does this thing with her tongue that undoes all my control. Blackness fills my vision as I come so hard in her mouth, I can barely stay standing.

"Good?" she whispers, standing in front of me.

I lift the hand that was between her legs and place her fingers in my mouth, exaggerating while I lick each finger, tasting her. A taste I've missed the past four days.

She runs her hands up my torso, dragging my shirt up until it goes over my head and falls to the floor. I tear off my briefs and step out of my pants.

"Get naked," I tell her, turning us so I can sit on the bed and watch her.

Her cheeks flush pink and her hands cross over her body, taking the hem of her sweater and pulling it off her body. I bite my lip from the view of her in a bra with her jeans wide open, revealing matching panties that I want to take off with my teeth. She unhooks her bra, wrapping a hand around her breasts as the straps fall to her shoulders.

"Let me see, baby," I whisper.

She opens her arms and the silk fabric falls to the floor. The weight of her perfect tits adjust down a bit, her nipples pebbled.

"Come here." I hold my arms out, needing to feel her, but she shakes her head, turning around and shimmying the jeans down past her ass, bending over in the process. "Fucking gorgeous."

Once she's out of her jeans, she teases me with her hands hooked into each side of her panties, pulling one side down, then the other.

"Do you wanna be punished?" I ask, a part of me hoping the answer is yes.

She giggles and pulls them down the rest of the way before turning around, completely nude. My dick is already hard again, needing no time to recover. She walks toward me and stands between my legs.

I run my hands from her hips up the sides of her abdomen until they rest just under her breasts. "Wanna play?"

She nods, her tongue sliding out.

I reach into my nightstand and grab the blindfold and rope. "Get on your back, hands and feet spread."

She does as I tell her, always so willing to trust me, and I place the blindfold over her eyes. I trail the silken rope over her body, letting it glide up her leg, past her slit, up her abdomen, being sure to brush the soft fabric over her nipples before I use it to secure both hands to the headboard.

She moans as I let my tongue trail a path down her body, purposely not dragging my tongue where I know she wants it most. Once her feet are tied open and secured to the footboard, I hold my weight over her body, my lips falling to hers in a promise of the ecstasy she's about to feel. My tongue slides down her torso, past her belly button, until I'm nestled between her legs.

"I love your beard." She wiggles under me.

I know this. She's told me many times that she loves the way the bristles scrape against her skin when I go down on her.

My tongue darts out of my mouth and I tease her with the tip along her folds, circling her clit. She bucks up and groans, trying to close her legs against the sensation but unable to because of the rope holding her open. I can tell that her hands want to dive into my hair by the way she keeps fisting and unfisting them.

I bring her to the brink over and over, moving from her clit to her opening with my tongue until I use my fingers to push into her. "You're soaked."

"Please, Kane. Please."

I give her pussy one last kiss and move up her body, my dick now at her opening. I circle and toy with her until she's begging before I slowly move inside her. Damn, she's so warm, so wet, so *mine*. She moans and arches her back off the mattress.

I thrust into her and back out, my lips casting kisses all over her skin. I palm her tits and make her nipples sharp as glass with my tongue. Although I love fucking her when she can touch me, there's something about tying her up and having her at my mercy that is so fucking hot. I think it's the fact that she gets off on giving me that power too. It makes me want to draw out our pleasure.

She says my name like a prayer.

"Right here, baby." I run my thumb over her lips, and she opens, accepting it, twirling her tongue around my finger. I thrust a little harder inside her and her teeth clamp down on my thumb. I pull it out and replace it with my mouth, needing to kiss her as we fall apart.

My arms slide under her torso and pull her body down as my hips drive into her. Sweat forms between us, and curses and moans fill the room. Her pussy clenches my dick so hard, I close my eyes and think of the game last night to divert my attention and make sure she comes before me.

Jana's body tenses under mine. I push into her a few more times, angling my dick up to hit her G-spot, and she falls apart in my arms. I come inside her with a bellow, holding myself in her wet heat.

We lie there until the waves of our orgasms retreat. Then I undo her feet and arms and push her blindfold up over her head. She smiles at me, making me feel like a rock star.

"Hi," she says.

"Hi."

I kiss her and get out of bed to grab a washcloth. I clean her up, then toss her one of my T-shirts while I grab my sweatpants.

"I'm starving now," I say.

She hops on my back, her legs straddling my waist. "Feed me."

"I thought I just did that."

She laughs, and her arms tighten around my neck as I walk us to the kitchen.

Life is good. Really fucking good.

CHAPTER 22

"Get a room, you two!"

Jana

"So, he's your boyfriend?" Paisley asks, sitting on my couch with her legs tucked under her.

"Yeah."

"Oh man. I'm so happy for you." She raises her glass of water, and I tap it with my glass of wine.

"Thanks. It's weird to think about, since I never thought I'd have a relationship with anyone, especially Kane. But it doesn't feel weird when we're together."

Her eyes light up. "Does this mean that maybe you've changed your mind about kids?"

I see the hope in her eyes. She's really starting to show now, and I know she'd like nothing more than for me to join her in this momentous stage of her life.

I shake my head. "Sorry."

"*Ugh.* I want us to raise them together. They could be best friends just like us."

I sip my wine and extend my legs. "Being someone's girlfriend and being someone's wife and the mother of their children is completely different."

She shrugs. "I just wish."

"I know, Pais, but I don't want them and neither does Kane, so it works for us."

"Kane doesn't want kids?" Her eyes practically bulge out.

"Have you seen him with Annabelle? I thought for sure he'd be into it."

I shake my head, not about to divulge why Kane feels that way, but it's probably a conversation we should have again. Just to make sure he feels the same now that things are moving forward.

"Huh," she says. "That really surprises me."

We sit in silence for a moment. Fear grips my heart that Kane said that, but maybe he didn't mean it or maybe he thinks he doesn't want them but will change his mind. Because my best friend is right—Kane would make an amazing father.

"Don't overthink things," Paisley says, knowing me better than I know myself sometimes.

"I'm not."

"You are. I can see it all over your face. Just enjoy this, Jana."

"What if he wants to get married?" I cringe at the thought of being a wife, but at the same time, maybe being Kane's wife doesn't sound that bad.

She sits up. "You've officially been his girlfriend for all of two days now. Calm down."

Paisley is right. My mind is messing with me. I need to just enjoy this.

"These are the fun days. The early stages when you can't get enough of each other and all you think about is him." Paisley smiles as though she remembers those days fondly.

"So where does that leave you now?"

Paisley shrugs. "Oh, I love Maks. But now I'm not so willing to watch sports with him. I go upstairs to watch my own television shows. We argue about who emptied the dishwasher last. Things just get normal."

I chew the inside of my cheek. That sounds awful and not fun at all.

"But we still have hot sex." She runs her hands over her stomach. "Obviously I wouldn't have this little nugget otherwise."

I nod, unconvinced.

"Oh shit, Jana, stop it. Surely you knew this early stage wouldn't last forever?"

"I've never been in a relationship before. The most is, like, five dates with that finance guy my dad set me up with."

"There are ups and downs in every relationship. Like, before my period, I want to strangle Maksim. But then my hormones level out, and I just want to snuggle up to him and never have him leave my side."

"Speaking of periods..." I do not want to discuss this relationship thing anymore because I can feel my anxiety rising with every word that comes out of her mouth.

"Did you not get yours? Maybe we *will* have babies."

I give her a "give me a break" look. "Pais, I've been on the pill forever."

She mumbles under her breath and makes a face.

"But I've had some spotting in between cycles, which has never happened before."

She waves me off. "I've had that before. I spotted the entire first month of this pregnancy. Scary as shit, but the gyno told me it's okay. Not that I'm saying you're pregnant. I'm just saying I wouldn't worry about it."

"I made an appointment with Dr. Winston, but she can't get me in for, like, a month. Isn't that crazy?"

"Not to sound elitist but I'm sure with your name and your bank account you can find someone to see you sooner."

I wave her off. "Probably but I like my doctor. I've seen

her since I was a teenager and I'm comfortable with her. I can wait. It's not like it's something major."

"Get pregnant and they make room for you." She smiles widely, touching her stomach again.

I'm excited for my best friend to have a baby. She deserves all the happiness in the world, but hopefully she'll understand parenthood isn't for everyone.

"A month doesn't sound so bad."

She laughs and I down my glass of wine.

AFTER WORK, I head over to Kane's.

We seem to spend a lot of time over there. More than my place, because of Rocky.

I ring the doorbell and I hear Rocky sniffing on the other side of the door. Kane opens the door, and he's shirtless with a pair of shorts slung low on his hips. I'm so busy admiring him that I don't notice Rocky jumping at me.

"Whoa, Rock!" Kane yells, but the dog already has his front two paws on my shoulders.

"Hey, Rocky, I have a gift for you."

"You got something for the dog?" Kane smiles as though he never expected me to warm up to his dog.

Turns out Rocky isn't all that bad. He's just a little too affectionate. Like the other night when we were watching a movie and he kept putting his nose under my hand to pet him.

"We have to go outside though." I take his paws off me and walk into Kane's house. I love the comfortable and cozy vibe, but maybe it's just because it's Kane's space that I like being here so much. All the natural wood and dark colors are so him.

"No kiss?" he asks when I pat his stomach and pass him.

I step backward and rise to my tiptoes, kissing him. "Hello."

His hand splays on my back to keep me in place and he lowers his mouth to kiss me more thoroughly. By the end, I'm breathless and wanting more.

"Hi," he whispers.

The three of us go outside. I pull a new ball out of my purse and throw it toward the ocean. Rocky runs off the porch and chases the ball.

Kane comes up behind me, wrapping his arms around my waist and placing his chin on my shoulder. "There's something very erotic about you bringing my dog a toy."

"I think you find most things I do highly erotic."

His arms tighten and I inhale a deep breath, relishing being near him again. But Paisley's words haven't stopped replaying in my head.

We watch Rocky pick up the ball and fling it in the air, chasing it in the other direction.

"Want to go for a walk?" Kane asks.

I turn my head, and he kisses my lips. "Sure."

We head toward Rocky, and Kane runs ahead of me and tosses the ball into the water. Rocky chases after it again.

After we fall in line together, Kane slides his fingers through mine. "Tell me."

I feel my forehead wrinkle. "Tell you what?"

"I can sense that something's up. What's going on in that head of yours?" He tugs me closer to the water and I step away from the cool water covering my feet.

"Nothing."

He raises his eyebrows.

I sigh. "Are you sure about the not having kids thing? I

mean, things are progressing between us and I just want to make sure we're on the same page."

He laughs and Rocky brings us the ball. Kane bends down to pick it up and throw it again. "We're on the same page. I told you, I would never want a kid to have a childhood like I had."

"But your dad dying in a work accident is rare. That doesn't happen every day."

"True. But there are car accidents, illnesses, and a million other things. No one thinks it can happen to them until it does."

I nod because he's right. "And what about marriage?"

He chuckles and steps in front of me, stopping us from walking. Rocky brings the ball back and sets it between our feet in the sand, sitting down and patiently waiting.

"Your mind is in overdrive, eh?"

"Eh?" I mock his Canadianism like I do every time the word slips from his mouth.

He rolls his eyes and tucks a strand of hair behind my ear. "Enjoy the moment."

"Rocky wants us to throw the ball," I say, but Kane doesn't move.

"What has you thinking so hard?" He wraps me up in his arms, which is the best place on earth.

I shrug and look down and off to the side. "Paisley was over, and she was saying how different things get after you've been together for a while."

"Uh-huh."

"Like how they argue about the dishwasher and stuff."

"Uh-huh." He ducks down to get me to look at him. "We argue now over much smaller things than that. But that's us. Besides, I love it when we fight until we fuck."

I smile because I do too. Sometimes I purposely pick a fight, but I'll never tell him that.

"But they watch television separately and stuff." My bottom lip juts out.

He nods and places his finger under my chin, urging me to look at him. "We'll take things slow, but just go with what this is telling you." He places his hand over my heart. "And stop listening to this." He moves his hand to my temple. "And it will turn out exactly how you want it to."

I rest my forehead on his chest, and he kisses the top of my head. I probably am overthinking everything. I need to just enjoy this moment because I haven't been myself this much ever and Kane pulls that out of me. He makes me feel as though it's okay to be exactly who I am, and he likes me anyway.

"Come on." He puts his arm around my shoulders and bends over to throw the ball to Rocky.

Rocky runs into the water and Kane pulls me toward the water's edge, but I refuse to go. He's stronger than me, so I have to dig my heels into the sand.

"I'm gonna get you wet," he says.

"I prefer when you do that in the bedroom."

He chuckles and I get free, running along the water's edge to get away from him. Rocky thinks I'm racing him and jumps in and out of the waves next to me.

"I'm going to get you." Kane chases me, but his ankle isn't one hundred percent, so it gives me a lead.

Right when we reach his house, his arm swings around my stomach and I fall to the sand, him on top of me. The waves dip under my back, getting me soaked. He stares at me for a moment and doesn't say anything.

I gently touch his face, his beard. "What are you thinking?"

"Just how lucky I am."

I can't help but smile when he says things like that.

"I'd be your boyfriend for the rest of my life and die a happy man. My heart knows it and that's all that matters."

The shift between us is happening, I feel it. It scares me at the same time as it thrills me because I'm not even close to being sick of Kane Burrows.

"You're amazing." My whispered words carry on the wind, but I know he hears me when the corners of his mouth tip up.

His eyes catch mine, then he lowers himself on me, our lips meeting. Rocky circles us and nudges his ball into the crook of my neck, running in circles around us again.

But we're lost in each other and oblivious to our surroundings until we hear Emma's voice. "Get a room, you two!"

I bury my head in Kane's neck, laughing. He lifts his arm and flips her off, which only makes me laugh harder.

"Now it's my turn to undress you." He gets up, holding out his hand. "How about a shower?"

"Sounds perfect."

We walk up to his house, hand in hand. I'm unsure what the future holds, but I try with all my might to live in the moment because this moment is pretty great.

CHAPTER 23

"I've heard rumors."
—Kane

Kane

We all knew the winning streak would come to an end eventually, and it did with a tremendous loss to Toronto right in our own arena. I'm sitting in my office, stewing over the 4–0 loss, pissed that we couldn't score one fucking goal. It was like they knew every one of our plays.

There's a knock on my office door and I assume it's a player. "Yeah?" The door opens a sliver and Jana peeks her head in. "Probably not the best time."

She comes in and shuts the door. "I figured I could cheer you up a little. We're still sitting number one in our division. Give yourself a break."

"This coming from you? I guess you really do have a soft spot for me."

She sits on the edge of my desk, and I slide out my chair, placing my hand on her hip to bring her between my legs. I wrap my arms around her middle and she holds me. She does make a loss a lot easier to take.

"We have to do the press conference." My voice is muffled against her abdomen.

"I know. But I'll be right next to you."

I tighten my arms and rest my chin on her stomach. My

heart pinches when I see the concern in her eyes for me. It's been a long fucking time since anyone worried about me.

She runs her fingernails through my hair and kisses my forehead. "It's just one game, baby."

"Baby?"

She hasn't used any pet names for me before, and I can't deny it sounds nice coming from her.

"I meant—"

"I like it," I say, and she exhales.

Oh, my little vault. So scared of opening up.

She places a leg on either side of me and lets her weight settle on me, straddling me in the chair. "How much time do we have?"

My hands mold to her ass. "At least enough for a make-out session."

"Perfect."

Our lips meet, and the loss is the last thing on my mind. Now all I can think about is getting Jana back to my house and fucking her until dawn. She grinds on my cock that's turning fully hard. I'm so lost in her, the commotion outside doesn't register until my office door opens.

"Oh, he's busy, Mr. Gerhardt."

Jana strips her lips off mine, looking over her shoulder. I quickly remove my hands from her ass when I see Mr. Gerhardt in the office doorway. Aiden's behind him, cringing and mouthing sorry.

"Dad!" Jana screeches, trying to get free from me, but her heel gets caught on the arm of my chair. As I try to catch her, she falls to the floor.

"Are you okay?" I whisper.

She's quick to her feet like a cat with nine lives.

"What the hell is going on in here?" Mr. Gerhardt steps

in and slams my door. A few trophies on my bookshelf rattle.

"Um..." Jana stammers and glances at me.

I stand, and Mr. Gerhardt's gaze darts to where my slacks are currently tented. I turn to adjust myself for a moment, then circle back to him. "I really like your daughter, sir."

"Jana?" He looks at her.

She turns her attention to me and slowly smiles. She takes my hand. "I really like Kane."

My chest feels as though it's swelling from the declaration to her dad. It's the first time I've heard her tell anyone besides me how she feels, and suddenly like seems like a ridiculous word. Like we're seventh graders.

It's a split-second decision, but I decide to just lay it all out there. I'm tired of keeping my feelings inside and worrying that if I confess to Jana how I really feel, she'll bolt. So I look back at her father and say, "Actually, sir, I love her."

"What?" Jana whispers, her eyes filling with tears. She shakes her head. "No, you don't."

I huff and stare into her eyes. "Yes, I do. I love you, Jana Gerhardt. So much that even one night away from you makes my heart ache. I love everything about you. Even your stubborn side."

"She gets that from me," Mr. Gerhardt says with amusement.

"And you don't have to tell me you feel the same. It's okay," I assure her, but she glances at her dad and back at me.

"I love you too. As much as it scares the crap out of me, I do. I love you." She places her hand on my cheek.

I lean in for a chaste kiss, wishing her dad wasn't here so I could really show her how I feel.

"Well." Mr. Gerhardt throws his hands in the air. "What am I supposed to say now?"

Jana tears her gaze from mine. "I'm sorry, Dad, I should've told you sooner. It's just we didn't know where this was going and—"

"It's okay, Jana. Your life is your life. But do you two really think you can work together?"

"Of course," Jana says. "We're both professionals."

"That's all that matters to me. If you guys are good, then I am too."

Jana rounds the desk and gives her dad a big hug. "Thank you for understanding."

"Jana, you could have told me. I'm not completely blind. Two people only bicker like you two when there are strong feelings underneath. I suspected this might happen."

"Really?" Jana glances back at me with surprise.

"Really. Now you two need to get to the press conference. And you don't owe them any explanation about the two of you if and when it comes up. Go about your lives. If they report on it, so what? But you don't have to answer to them."

Jana kisses her dad's cheek. "Thank you."

He nods, and on my way to the door, I put my hand out for Mr. Gerhardt to shake. He slides his hand in mine and eyes me the way only a father can. His look says that if I don't take good care of his daughter, I have him to answer to. I nod, and it's a promise that he can trust me with her heart.

Jana and I walk out of my office and down the hall to the pressroom, hand in hand.

"Relieved?" I ask before we go in.

"Yeah, but did you mean it?"

I chuckle and press her back to the wall, my hand on her cheek. "I love you, Jana, and I'll keep saying it until you believe it."

She melts into me, which is always so much sweeter when you're dealing with someone who prides herself on being stoic.

OUR FIRST PUBLIC outing is a charity event that Mr. Gerhardt is sponsoring at his house. We've gone out for coffee and breakfast, but honestly, we just enjoy being at my house, so there's been no reason for us to try to out ourselves. We're going to make a splash when we reveal our relationship today, and I'm sure it will make its way to the press.

I wasn't nervous about telling the world we're together until I looked at the mansion in front of us. It's a stark reminder of how different we grew up. It's easy to just see Jana as Jana when we're hanging out at my place, but this is something else.

"This is where you grew up, right?" I stare at the monstrosity in front of me.

"I'm going to take you to the orange orchard," she whispers as her arm slides through mine, and I get the sense she might be a little nervous too.

"I've heard rumors."

I can't help but allow a little bit of doubt to creep inside me. Am I enough for Jana Gerhardt, heir to everything Gerhardt owns? The man has his own plane, his own helicopter, and a damn orange orchard on his property. I come from absolutely nothing.

We walk in the front doors and her parents are the first to greet us.

"Kane," her mom coos, hugging me. "I heard the wonderful news. I wish Jana would've let me have you two over for dinner. She says you're always so busy."

Jana sighs next to me. "Well, I am the owner and he's the coach of a hockey team that's currently a contender for the Cup."

"A few hours for a dinner isn't the end of the world, Jana." Her mom kisses her cheek. "You look stunning."

Her mom couldn't be more right. Jana's wearing red. A fucking red dress, red heels, and red lipstick, and my dick's been hard since I picked her up.

"I said the same, Mrs. Gerhardt." I smile at Jana and her cheeks pinken.

"Charlotte, please," her mom says, looking over our shoulders. "Go, you two. Enjoy your evening. And after you win that Cup, the first line of business is for you to come here."

Jana groans. "We will, Mother."

The two of us step into the main room where two bars have been set up.

"What do you want to drink?" I ask.

"Just a white wine." She waves to her friends in the corner.

"I'll bring it to you." I kiss her cheek, and I catch a few people noticing.

I head toward the bar where Aiden, Ford, and Warner are.

"She had this crying fit over mascara. These hormones are crazy fuckers," Warner says as I approach.

"Lena hasn't been pregnant yet. We're waiting for Annabelle to get older. But now you have me terrified." Ford drinks his beer.

I eavesdrop while I order our drinks.

"Saige isn't even pregnant, and the other day, I'm watching March Madness and she starts picking up my plate on the coffee table and telling me this isn't a frat house. Last March Madness, she did a bracket with me, and we hung out at a bar the entire time. Some of the late-night games, we were in bed naked. What a difference a year makes."

That sounds like it sucks. Jana would never do that. Then again, Aiden didn't think Saige would either.

"Hey, boys," I say.

"You're still in the bubble, so you can't join in." Warner clinks his glass with Aiden and Ford.

"Where's Maksim?"

"He's in the bathroom. Paisley's not feeling great."

I nod and go deliver the drink to Jana, and she thanks me with a kiss. "Ladies," I say, but I overhear the women complaining about the men.

This is the last thing either of us needs after we just told each other we loved each other a couple weeks ago.

Heading back toward the boys, I decide at the last minute to head outside, not wanting to hear them complaining about the women in their lives.

The sky is dark over the Gulf, only a sliver of the moon casting a trickle of light. I sip my drink and clasp it in two hands, wondering what it would be like to live in a house like this as a little kid.

"You're Kane Burrows, right?" A man comes up to me, putting out his hand. "Ty Irving. I went to school with Jana."

I shake his hand. "Good to meet you."

"I hate to be forward, but I have a question for you... are the two of you a couple?"

The guy has his blond hair swept to the side, and his thin figure—which reminds me more of a runner's body— doesn't do a lot for his tuxedo. Then again, the fact that he's asking me about my girlfriend has my defenses up, so maybe I'm biased.

"Yes, we're together."

His head rocks back and disappointment flashes across his face. "I thought so. I only came tonight to see her, then I saw you two when you delivered her drink. Figured it was more than just boss and employee." He laughs. I don't. "Good luck, man. Although I'll warn you, she's not really a long-term kind of girl."

"I don't need luck. And maybe she just hadn't met the right person." I arch an eyebrow.

He pats my shoulder in a condescending move. If we weren't at the Gerhardts', his ass would be on the ground by now. "That's what all the ones before you thought too."

I shake my head, and he heads down the outside stairs. I overhear him talking to someone else.

"Yeah, Jana's banging him. Can you believe it? Her standards sure have fallen."

Usually, what some spoiled prick of a rich kid thinks wouldn't bother me, but this guy is definitely under my skin.

"There you are." Jana's voice pulls me from my thoughts, and I turn to find her walking toward me.

"Just met a friend of yours." I tip my drink to my lips.

She doesn't stop until she's in my arms, and I hold her close for a moment longer than normal. "Who?"

"Ty Irving?"

Her scowl is immediate. "He's such an asshole, so I'll apologize now for whatever he said to you."

I kiss her temple. "No need."

And I mean it. I love this woman. I'm the one who's slowly pulling her out of her shell and allowing her to feel safe and comfortable to be who she is. Oh, and I'm the first man she's ever loved besides her father, so Ty Irving can go fuck himself.

CHAPTER 24

"Don't answer that."
—Kane

Jana

I pick up my phone and see I'm due at the doctor's office in an hour. "Crap!"

"What?" Kane rolls over, his arm slapping where I was just lying in his bed. "Come back."

"I have to get to the doctor." I run into his bathroom, stripping my clothes off as I go.

Rocky picks up his head from his dog bed, but he lies back down when he sees I'm not leaving the room.

"Doctor? Did I know about this?" Kane follows me into the bathroom and rests his hip on the vanity.

"Didn't I tell you?"

He tenses. "No. Is there something I need to know?"

I turn on the water in the shower, put my hand under the spray, and shut the glass door since it's still too cold. The one disadvantage of Kane's house is his crappy water heater.

"No, just you know how occasionally there's some blood when we..." I don't finish because he should understand.

"And?"

"And that shouldn't be happening. I've started to bleed a bit between periods, and I'm not sure if it's the pill or whatever."

"But you're not..."

I shake my head. "No, I'm not pregnant."

Finally, the water is hot enough for me to go in. I get under the water and quickly shampoo my hair, feeling his eyes on me through the fogged-up glass. "Kane, there's nothing wrong."

"If there was nothing wrong, you wouldn't be going to the doctor."

"True, but this isn't life or death or pregnancy. This is just my body reacting to something. Maybe too much sex." I wipe my hand over the condensation and wink through the glass, but he remains silent.

"I'm going with you."

"No, you're not." I shake my shaving cream container and find it empty. "Can I borrow some shaving cream?"

"Is this doctor a man or woman?"

"Woman."

"Either way, why do you have to shave to see them?"

I open the door and a rush of steam pours through the crack. He hands me the can of shaving cream. I'm not sure the last time he used it.

"Because I'm going to have to spread my legs for her, and I want to make sure I look good."

"Babe, you look good. No worries on the primping."

"Good hygiene isn't primping," I say, running the razor up my leg the fastest I can.

"I'd still like to go with you."

I stick my head out while conditioner sits in my hair. "It's just a checkup, and the whole thing is uncomfortable as it is. Plus, you have practice."

He nods. The head coach can't just take time off because his girlfriend is having period problems. "Call me after."

"I'm coming to the office after."

"Perfect, I'll come see you." He leaves the room and whistles for Rocky to follow him.

I finish getting ready, lotion up my legs and body, put on a wrap dress and a pair of heels. I've started keeping some of my things here at Kane's since I spend so much time here. It's just easier.

After I'm ready, I have about fifteen minutes to get there and it's ten minutes away.

"I made you an egg sandwich." Kane hands me something wrapped in foil. "Here's your coffee." He puts a to-go mug of his on the counter.

I take the time to kiss him. "Thank you."

"You're welcome. Let me know when you're done?"

"Of course."

I snatch the sandwich and the coffee, shaking my head over how we became so domesticated so fast. Him making me a to-go breakfast and looking so concerned because I'm going to the doctor. Regardless, it feels like a safety net around me, and I don't hate it.

"Bye, Rocky." I pet his head, and he wags his tail.

Kane watches out the front door as I pull out of the driveway. I speed down the street, knowing if I'm too late, they won't let me see the doctor.

WHY DO I rush to these appointments? You always end up waiting way past your appointment time, regardless of what time you arrive.

A half an hour *after* my appointment time, a nurse opens the door and everyone looks up, hoping their name will be called. Lucky for me, she calls my name. I practically jump up because it's as if I won the lottery. Especially when all the pregnant people in the office made me feel like the room was closing in.

The nurse, Helen, weighs me and takes me to a room where she asks me why I'm here. We go over the spotting and how I'm on the pill and sexually active. She gives me a gown and says Dr. Winston will be right in.

I hurry to change before the dreaded knock on the door. For some reason, I'm always afraid I won't undress in time, but then I end up on the chair/lounger thing forever, thinking they forgot about me.

Busying myself with my phone, I scroll through Instagram to see all my friends living their best lives. I type in Kane's name to see if he's added anything personal to his profile, but there's only a picture of Rocky. Other than that, it's just professional things.

A knock on the door has me putting my phone down on my abdomen.

"Come in," I say, and Dr. Winston walks in with a wide smile. A nurse follows her in and goes to sit in the chair in the corner.

"Jana, how are you?" She goes to the computer and scans her badge.

"Hey, Dr. Winston, I'm okay."

"Running a hockey team must not be easy. I hope you're doing something to release the stress."

I laugh, and she looks at me. "Oh yeah. I'm fine."

I explain to her about my periods, and she listens to my concerns, typing them in my chart on the computer.

"Well, this pill has always worked for you, but sometimes things change. Let's do some blood tests and check your hormones. Maybe we'll try another pill. First, let's do an exam and get a PAP test to make sure there are no concerns there."

She makes conversation about the players while she does my exam and tells me how much she loves Warner, especially the pictures he shares of him and his son on Instagram.

"Are they all taken now?" she asks.

"Most of our team are in committed relationships. I had no idea you were a hockey fan."

She laughs. "I'm not a hockey fan. I just like hockey players. Speaking of, I heard a rumor about the coach... but you don't have to answer."

I chuckle. "It's true."

She peeks up from between my legs with a huge smile. "I kind of miss watching him play. He always made stopping those pucks look so easy."

"Yeah, I think he might miss it too."

She slides out from between my legs, removes her gloves, then offers me her hand and helps me to sit back up. "Everything looks good. Go ahead and get dressed. I'll send the nurse in for a blood draw, and we'll send it in to the lab. Someone will call you with the results in a few days, and we'll go from there."

"Okay, thanks."

"My suspicion is you may just need a higher dose since you're having break-through bleeding, but this will give us a good direction to go in." She leaves the room.

Again, I feel like it's a race to get dressed so I don't moon the poor nurse.

I shoot Kane a quick text since he seemed so concerned earlier.

Me: *Getting bloodwork for answers. Doctor isn't concerned.*

Kane: *Good news.*

I stuff my phone into my purse, and the nurse comes in

and takes five vials of blood. I wonder why she needs that much. When I leave the office, I find everyone at the front desk is extra smiley and whispering to one another. I think Dr. Winston might have a big mouth.

It only takes me a half hour to get to the office, and when I arrive, Barbara hands me a stack of handwritten messages. I read through them while I walk to my desk and sit in my chair, but I can't concentrate on work.

Something just feels off, but I can't put my finger on it.

An hour later, I hear Kane outside my office. "Morning, Barbara, no interruptions."

He walks in, shuts the door, and locks it. My head tilts.

"What are you doing?" My phone rings as soon as the words leave my mouth.

"Don't answer that."

I glance at my phone. "It's Imogen."

"Don't answer."

There's a knock on the door. "Kane, I saw you go in there. Barbara, call into her office, please." It's Imogen outside my office now.

"What's going on? Is she trying to get you to do that piece for *Sports Illustrated*?" I ask.

He stands at the door like a bodyguard. "No, I told her I'd do that, and that's when she tried to trick me."

My desk phone rings, and I pick it up. "Hello, Barbara."

"Imogen Jacobs-Langley would like to talk to you."

"Please send her in." I look across the room at my boyfriend. "Kane, get away from the door."

"Trust me when I say you do not want her to come in here." He looks so serious, I want to laugh. Like he's a little kid who got caught doing something bad and is hiding from his parents.

"What's with you? Let the poor woman in."

"You asked for it." He unlocks the door and walks farther into the office.

"Send Imogen in," I tell Barbara.

The door opens and Imogen walks in, scowling at Kane as she sits in the chair in front of my desk. "Hi, Jana. I love that dress on you."

"Stop kissing up," Kane says, standing off to the side with his arms crossed.

I turn to him. "I like to think I do look good in this dress."

"You look smokin', baby. But Imogen has ulterior motives." He motions for Imogen to carry on with whatever she has to say.

She looks over her shoulder and gives him a scathing glare.

"What is going on here?"

"Well, so... um... my sister, Morgan, is a bit of an artist, and she has a big gallery spot that her professor sets up for all his students, but kids can't go. As you know, Paisley hasn't been feeling great, and Saige and Aiden planned a quick getaway. Cory's parents happen to be coming that night to look for a place in the area and..."

I look at Kane, and he's waving his hands behind her, mouthing no while shaking his head.

"Are you asking us to babysit Jalen?"

She looks over her shoulder at Kane and back at me. "And Annabelle." She puts her hands in front of her in prayer pose. "I promise I'll have everything ready to go, and Jalen is sleeping like a dream. Annabelle loves Kane. We won't be far. If something happens, we could come right back. It's just, I don't trust anyone else really."

I lean back in my chair. "I'm not sure if I should be offended you asked me last or not."

"It wasn't that. I just didn't want to bother you. I figure you and Kane have a lot on your plate, especially with the team so close to playoffs. I wouldn't even ask, but Morgan is so excited, and she'll be heartbroken if we all can't be there."

"I'd be happy to do it." I look at Kane, who rolls his eyes. "*We'll* be happy to help. When is it?"

"Next week. Thursday night."

I grab my phone and enter it in my calendar. "Done. Are we doing this at your house or Ford's?"

"Ford's. Only because I'll bring the Pack 'n Play over there for Jalen, and Annabelle is used to sleeping in her crib." She stands with a huge smile. "Thank you so much, Jana!" She comes around and hugs me tightly. Then she walks toward the door. "Kane." Her tone is full of annoyance, then she leaves my office.

The minute the door shuts, Kane says, "What are you thinking?"

"We're doing our friends a favor."

After all, just because we don't want kids, that doesn't necessarily mean we can't be the fun aunt and uncle, right?

CHAPTER 25

"Remember you asked us."
—Kane

Kane

"Mom's in the hospital," Lee says the second I finish saying hello.

I lean back in the couch and scratch my beard. "How about a hey, how are ya before you slam me with that news? And why am I finding out from you? Aunt Sarah should be calling me." I mute the game tape.

"Because I'm off-season and your team is heading into finals."

"Oh, that's right, you couldn't make it to the Super Bowl."

He groans. I wish hearing my mom was in the hospital caused more of a panic for me, but the truth is, she's been in and out of our lives ever since my dad died. She'll periodically go off her meds and refuse to go see her therapist. It's a vicious cycle.

It scared the crap out of me when I was younger, but it's been so many years of the same thing over and over that I think I'm numb to the news.

"I'm flying up to see her, then I'm coming to you. Figure I'm gonna stay in Florida until you win the Cup."

"Don't go putting that kind of pressure on me," I tell him. "You're gonna jinx it."

"You fucking hockey players and your superstitions." I can practically see him shaking his head at me.

"Football players have them too. Every athlete does, whether they admit it or not." I get up and grab a beer from the fridge. "I should probably go see her. We have two days off."

"It's up to you. I understand if you don't want to. Maybe you want to invite Jana up?"

Hmm... I'm not sure about that. Jana seeing where I grew up and how fucked up my family is? No thanks. Especially now that I've seen where she grew up.

"What did the doctor say?" I figure the severity will dictate what I need to do.

"Aunt Sarah said the doctor wants her back on her meds and he'd like her to go through therapy. She's in the psych ward on a seventy-two-hour hold before she'll be released. The usual."

"Will they let us see her?" I take a pull off my beer.

"I'm not sure."

I'm torn. I feel as though I should go see her, but I spent much of my youth visiting her in the hospital. It wouldn't kill Lee to take the lead on this one. I love my mom and I want to help her, but I realized a long time ago that there's actually not much I can do for her besides make sure she has access to the doctors and treatment options she needs. As heartbreaking as that is.

I'm in the middle of getting my team to the finals and winning the Cup. I have responsibilities here I can't shuck off. "Yeah, I'm not going."

"Cool. I'll go represent, but then I'm coming to you."

"Awesome. Give Mom my best. I'll call her once she's out."

I say goodbye to my brother and sit back on my couch,

drinking my beer and staring at the picture that's frozen on my television. I fidget, unable to get situated, and decide that instead of watching tape, I'm going for a walk.

I whistle for Rocky. "Come on, boy."

He barrels over to me, picks up his ball, and breezes through the French doors. Outside, I wave to Emma and Sam enjoying an early dinner on their deck, then throw the ball for Rocky, restless in my own skin.

I always get this way when it comes to my mom. The feeling that I should be doing more is pervasive, but I know from experience that I can't let it overtake my entire life.

By the time Rocky and I make it back to my place, my mind isn't any more settled, but warmth spreads through my chest when I spot Jana sitting on the sand behind my house, staring out at the water. Rocky ignores his ball and runs over to her, so rambunctious Jana ends up on her back while he licks her face. My dog has excellent taste.

"Hey, I wasn't expecting you," I say, lying down next to her and staring at the sky.

"Is it a problem that I'm here?"

I link my hands with hers on the sand. "Never. You're welcome anytime."

She turns to me and gives me a sweet smile that doesn't reach her eyes. Something's going on. Although it doesn't look like she was crying, she looks as though she's on the brink.

"What's wrong?"

"Nothing." She sits up and crosses her legs, allowing the sand to slip through her fingers.

I sit up beside her. "Try again."

"The doctor called with my blood test results." She continues letting the sand stream through her fingers.

Rocky brings his ball over to her and drops it where

she's playing. She picks it up and throws it in the water, and he rushes off.

"And?"

"She's changing my pills."

"That's good, right?"

She nods.

"But?"

"Something else showed up in my bloodwork." She swallows. "Nothing bad, so don't worry."

"But it upset you." My chest tightens, making it hard to breathe.

"It shouldn't. I'm just surprised. I'm still processing it."

"Do you want to tell me?" The thing with Jana is I'm always afraid that if I push too hard, she'll bolt.

"I'm starting to go through perimenopause. My hormones... although I don't understand any of it, apparently my results tell the doctor that I'm one of those women who will go through menopause at an earlier than normal age."

"Oh." I'm a complete dumbass for not thinking of something better to say to make her feel better, but she didn't want to have kids, so I'm not sure why she's so upset.

"It's just so final. You know? Not to mention all the other shit that goes along with it—none of it pleasant." She blows out a long breath. "It might sound stupid, but it makes me feel... old. I don't know. The not having kids thing is just one part of it."

Fucking hell, what a day. First my mom and now this. "Does it change things for you?"

She's quick to shake her head.

Relief washes through me.

"No, I still don't want kids. But it was my choice, and

pretty soon it won't be my choice, you know? What if I change my mind in three years? Will it be too late?"

"That makes it sound like you're unsure about your decision."

She glares at me. "No, Kane, it means I'm upset because the choice is being taken away from me."

I hold up both my hands. "I'm not the enemy here. Let's remember, you didn't want to date me because you thought *I* wanted kids." I hate the anger in my voice, so I force myself to calm down. "I'm sorry. I don't mean to get upset."

"No. You're right. But you can relax. I'm not switching up the game. I just... I don't know... I don't know why I feel this way." Her head tips down and a tear drops from her eye to the sand below.

I wrap my arm around her, and Rocky comes over, putting his head in her lap, and she pets him. We sit there until the sun descends, allowing her to grieve something she didn't think she wanted.

THE DAY I've been dreading arrives. The babysitting day. Jana has perked up a little since the call from her doctor. I'm pretty sure it was just shock about the news and nothing more. Mom is back home, and we've spoken. She sounds halfway decent, but Aunt Sarah is going to stay with her for a while. Lee plans to stick around there until we get the playoff schedule.

"I cannot believe you got us into this," I say for the millionth time as Jana and I stand outside Ford's house.

"You know what? If you don't want to be here, then go. I'll do it myself."

I step back, surprised by her anger. "I just meant—"

"We're doing it, Kane, so suck it up or go home."

I cock my head, blinking at Jana for a moment until Lena opens the door, a look of sympathy already on her face. "Thank you both for coming. We so appreciate it. I promise we won't be long. Ford's dad said something about drinks, but I told Ford absolutely not."

"It's okay, Lena, stay out as long as you want," Jana says.

"Well, come in." She opens the door farther and motions for us to step inside.

We walk in and Annabelle runs to us immediately, clinging to my leg. "Swim!"

"No, Annabelle, I told you no." Lena shakes her head.

Annabelle stares for a beat longer than I would think an almost-three-year-old would and stomps away.

"Don't let her swindle you into it either. We've fed her, so just some snacks if she gets hungry. Believe it or not, she knows the stations for her favorite TV shows. Bedtime is at eight, and she likes a story read to her. Make sure the monitor is on, shut the door, and we'll be home not too long after. I'm hoping it all goes smoothly."

Ford walks down the stairs in a custom-tailored suit and flashes us his classic smile. "Got suckered into it, huh? I knew putting my sister in charge of recruitment was the right move."

"When you get moved down to second line, you'll know why," I mumble, sitting down to help Annabelle with a puzzle.

"We're here! So sorry we're late. It was a nightmare getting out of the house." Imogen walks in with Jalen in a carrier, and Warner's arms are overloaded with things. Imogen puts Jalen down, then takes the Pack 'n Play out of Warner's hands and sets it up in the corner of the room. "He can sleep in here. I've packed him three sets of pajamas. I hope that's enough."

"Aren't we only watching him for one night?" I ask.

"Yes, but sometimes the diaper doesn't keep everything in." Imogen gives Jana an apologetic look.

I growl.

"My breast milk is here." She holds up some bags and my eyes widen. "I'll put them in the fridge. Feed him, burp him, and put him down. He's been sleeping great, so crossing my fingers it's all okay tonight."

"So, we're going to cross our fingers and hope? Good to know," I grumble.

Jana glares over her shoulder at me, as she should. I'm being an ass tonight.

"We left you money for food on the coffee table," Ford chimes in.

"We're not fifteen. We can take care of our own food," Jana says.

Ford moves his hand to take the money back.

"Leave the money, Ford," I say, and he lifts his hand and holds it up. I'm not paying for my own dinner.

"Well, you all look gorgeous," Jana says. "Now go have fun. We'll be fine."

Lena and Ford crouch to kiss Annabelle, telling her they love her.

"You know she'll never remember this, right? Like, in the span of her life, you guys being away for a few hours is nothing."

They both give me the same look as Jana. So yeah, I'm the designated asshole in the room for the evening.

Warner takes Jalen out of the carrier, and he and Imogen coo and tell the little guy how much they love him. Then they hand him over to Jana, who holds him out from her body by his armpits.

"What are you doing?" Warner asks. He looks at Imogen. "What is she doing?"

"Jana, sweetie, you can hold him like this." Imogen takes Jalen out of Jana's hands and lays him in her arms. "He likes that position more."

Jana looks at the little baby, her entire body filled with tension. Maybe now she's getting why I didn't want to be here tonight. "Oh yeah, okay."

The four of them look scared shitless to leave.

I raise my hand. "Remember you asked us. Not the other way around."

"Kane!" Jana scolds. "We'll be fine. Promise. I'll call if there's even the slightest hiccup."

"Okay, you need us, call us," Imogen singsongs before the door shuts behind them.

"I thought they were never going to leave." I say to Annabelle, and she laughs as though she understands me. "What do you want to do?"

"Swim!"

"Cool, go get your swimsuit," I tell her.

"Didn't you hear Lena?" Jana asks.

"The little girl wants to swim. I don't see the harm in it."

Annabelle runs up the stairs.

"Well then, you better go follow her."

I head toward the stairs, Jana watching me the entire time.

"And people wonder why I don't want kids," I mumble.

By the time I get to her room, Annabelle is in a drawer, throwing her swimsuits on the floor. She picks out a striped one and begins undressing. I turn around to face the other direction

"She's stripping down. I don't think I should see this," I yell down to Jana.

"First of all, she's undressing, not stripping, Kane! And she's two. You're fine."

Turns out I only have to help Annabelle get her arms through the straps of her bathing suit. I go to help her with her socks, but she's quick to turn around to do it herself.

Jesus, it starts this young with women thinking men can't do anything right?

CHAPTER 26

Jana

Kane returns with Annabelle in his arms, and she's babbling about water, swimming, cold.

Jalen is asleep in the Pack 'n Play, so I follow them to the pool, leaving the patio door open a crack so I can hear if Jalen wakes.

"Are you going to borrow one of Ford's swimsuits?" I ask Kane.

Annabelle goes to the bin and picks out her floaty, then drops it on the edge of the water. Then she goes back to the bin and grabs a few toys and sits down on the steps, playing with them.

"She's pretty smart," Kane says, sounding impressed.

"Uh-huh." I still watch her, although I'm guessing Lena and Ford must've taught her she can't just go in the pool. "Again, what are you going to wear in the pool?"

Kane looks at me. "I'm not wearing another man's swimsuit, I can tell you that." He strips off his shirt and takes off his shorts.

"Kane!"

"What? My boxer briefs are like a swimsuit. Think of the guys who wear speedos."

I guess I understand his point, so I watch him hop in the

shallow end and hold his hands out for Annabelle to jump in. She instantly abandons her toys and jumps at him.

"Float!" she screams.

"Annabelle, Jalen is sleeping. Let's be a little quieter." I put my finger to my lips, and she nods.

Kane positions her on her back while still holding her up. Slowly, he gets his hand out from underneath her and she floats with her arms and legs outstretched, her eyes squeezed shut. He claps after a little while and she flips over and treads water for a second until Kane picks her up. He praises her and her face lights up, then he throws her and she squeals.

I hear the baby start crying inside.

So much for Jalen sleeping.

"Whoops, we woke Jalen." Kane cringes at Annabelle, but neither of them seems concerned.

I leave the pool and pick up Jalen, whose face is completely red from screaming. Where is that cute little boy from the Instagram pictures?

"Oh, you poor thing," I say, realizing he's wet all the way through his onesie.

I didn't want to ask Imogen for a diaper lesson because I thought it would scare her. I've never changed a baby's diaper, nor have I fed a baby, but I watched a few YouTube videos before I came over. Kane was so against babysitting tonight that the competitive demon inside me said we can do this. Plus, I want to help Paisley when her daughter is born. I might not want to be called Mom, but I do want the label best aunt ever.

I dig through the designer diaper bag and find a new onesie, a diaper, diaper cream, and wipes. While Kane is still outside, I pull up the YouTube video and lay Jalen on the upper portion of the Pack 'n Play to change him. He's actually calmed down now and staring at the ceiling.

"Hey, little one." My fingers tiptoe up his stomach and I unsnap all the buttons on the onesie.

I must say, to my surprise, I kinda feel like a natural. The onesie comes off, I take off the old diaper, wipe him down, apply diaper rash cream, and put on a new diaper.

"Whoa, check me out," I whisper to Jalen. It might take me a long time, but I get him all snapped into a new onesie. "Good as new, little man." I swoop him up and go back out to the pool. "Look who's up."

Annabelle looks over and turns back to Kane. "Catch me!"

She jumps in the water. Kane brings her back over to the edge. I sit on the opposite edge of the pool with Jalen in my arms.

"Sorry for waking him," Kane says, coming over and letting Jalen wrap his little fingers around Kane's big pointer finger. "Amazing how small they are, eh? To think I was this size once."

I laugh. "I know." It's hard to picture this big burly man ever being this helpless.

"Kane! Kane!" Annabelle screams from the other side. "Catch me."

She jumps in without Kane being there to catch her. He rushes over and gets her just as she's going down.

Once she's back up and in his arms, he tells her, "You can't do that. I have to know you're going to jump, and I need to be there."

"Stop playing with Jalen," she says.

Kane glances over his shoulder at me. I've never seen this side of Annabelle, but I guess before Jalen, she was the only child in the family and used to getting all the attention.

"You know what? I'm going to go fix his bottle. Do you want a snack, Annabelle? We could watch a movie."

"One more jump," she says.

I leave them and put Jalen in the bouncer. One of the many things Warner had to bring tonight. Imogen is just as organized as I would be if I were a mom, so she's left clear directions for the bottle. I test the bottle on my wrist like I saw in the YouTube video, then go over to the bouncer.

"Open up, little guy." I bring the bottle to his lips, but he doesn't open them. He just stares at me.

"How's it going?" Kane has a towel wrapped around his waist with Annabelle right next to him and wrapped in a ladybug towel of her own.

I do a double take because watching the two of them makes my heart flip.

"I know we're tracking in water. I'll clean up once I have her all set." Kane picks her up, towel and all.

"Oh, I know." My voice is quiet as I try to make sense of this foreign feeling inside me.

They disappear upstairs and I continue to attempt to give Jalen the bottle, but it's a no go. He will not open his mouth.

"You're stubborn like your uncle Kane. I got cocky, so you're putting me in my place, huh?" I laugh, and he kicks both of his feet, staring at the bottle as though he wants it. "Then come on." I run the nipple of the bottle over his lips again.

Jalen gets more antsy as my anxiety increases.

"Hold him," Annabelle says when they come back downstairs, witnessing my almost breakdown. "He fuzzy."

I think she means fussy, and I hold back my laugh. Her hair is still wet.

I meet Kane's gaze. "They're going to smell the chlorine on her."

He holds up his hands. "I draw the line at giving her a bath."

"Well." I signal to Jalen then unstrap him and cradle him in my arms.

Sure enough, he accepts the bottle immediately.

"You're a smart girl," I say to Annabelle, and she smiles and goes to the television.

"Movie?" she asks me.

"After I finish with Jalen, I'm going to give you a bath, Annabelle," I say and her face lights up. "So maybe just a short show first?"

Kane goes for the remote, but Annabelle climbs on his lap and takes the remote, pressing the buttons. Sure enough, a kid show comes on.

"Man, that boy is hungry," Kane says.

For a moment, I can't do anything but stare at him and Annabelle. She's tucked into his arms, leaning on her side. There goes my heart again.

Thankfully, Jalen finishes his bottle, and I put him on my shoulder, lightly patting his back. When a huge belch comes out, my excitement comes out with a squeal. "I did it."

Annabelle looks at me as though I'm boring, and Kane looks as though he doesn't understand why I'm so excited.

"Awesome, babe," he says.

I stand. "We need to switch them, Mr. I Don't Give Baths."

"I'll give you a bath anytime." His eyes drag up and down my body, and my skin heats under his gaze.

"Behave," I scold him.

"Bath?" Annabelle perks up.

The girl definitely has some profession with water in her future.

We switch kids, and I'm a little surprised by how easily Kane takes Jalen from my arms.

Upstairs, I pick up Annabelle's wet swimsuit from the floor of her room and ask her to pick out some pajamas. She goes to her drawer and grabs a unicorn onesie I know will make her look adorable. Then we go into the bathroom, and I shut the door and turn on the water. This I can handle. Kane's wet boxer briefs are lying on the edge of the tub, so I take those and put them aside to put in a plastic bag and then in my purse.

The bath is a lot of fun. Annabelle plays in the water and is pretty self-sufficient. Maybe that comes from being an only child. I wash and condition her hair, and she doesn't complain. The whole experience is pretty relaxing. Why was I so afraid of this?

I get her dressed in her pajamas, and we come downstairs to find Jalen asleep on Kane's chest. There's that feeling again, and I absently rub my sternum.

"You okay?" Kane asks, forehead wrinkled, eyes assessing.

"I think I have heartburn. We haven't eaten anything."

He stands and puts Jalen in the bouncer. "I could go out and grab something?"

Annabelle heads to the couch and changes the channel back to her show. Definitely an only child.

"I'm sure we can find something here. Plus, they said they wouldn't be too long." I look at the clock. I can't believe it's already been so long. Time just races by when you're taking care of kids apparently.

Kane and I go into the kitchen and look in the fridge and the pantry for food. Annabelle is singing along with some intro song of a show she must love. I find some cheese and crackers, and Kane decides to make popcorn and grabs some of Annabelle's puff snacks.

I turn around from the pantry and tell Annabelle, "Kane is going to bring you some snacks."

I come around the other side of the large island and return to the family room and look around, not seeing Jalen in the bouncer anywhere. My adrenaline spikes and my pulse skyrockets.

I circle around. "Annabelle? Where's Jalen?"

She shrugs and continues watching her show, not even bothering to look at me.

The bouncer and Jalen are gone. Oh my god. I press a hand to my stomach. I think I might vomit.

"Annabelle, where is he?" I ask again with a sterner voice.

"He wanted quiet."

"No. No, he didn't. *Kane!*" I bend down to her level, blocking her view of the TV screen.

Kane rushes over. "What's up?" His hand is already in the popcorn and he's shoveling it in his mouth.

"Jalen is gone, and Annabelle says he wanted quiet." I try to keep the panic out of my voice.

Kane's eyes widen. "Okay. Okay."

"Not okay," I snap.

Kane bends down in front of Annabelle beside me, and I decide to start looking. There's nowhere far she could have gone with him. I check the door to the pool to make sure the child guard is on. It is.

"Annabelle, we need to know where Jalen is?" Kane asks her in a calm voice.

"Shh…" She puts her finger to her mouth.

"Jalen?" I call, clapping.

"He's not a dog, Jana," Kane says, realizing Annabelle is going to give us nothing.

I become frantic and go through everything from behind the couches to the Pack 'n Play .

"We lost their baby," I say, pushing my hands through my hair, near tears.

"He's here. He can't walk."

Annabelle acts oblivious, watching her show.

I open the bathroom door and fall to my knees in relief. Cute little Jalen is in here, fast asleep. "Found him, Kane."

He comes in and gives me a look like, What the hell? He bends down and picks up Jalen, bouncer and all. Annabelle must have dragged the bouncer in here.

"Annabelle, that isn't funny," I tell her.

She ignores us and picks up her snack. "Movie?"

Again, Kane and I share a look like, What the fuck?

A half hour later, the house has quieted down. Annabelle is asleep with her head on my lap, and I'm running my hands through her hair while Jalen is asleep in his Pack 'n Play. The front door creaks open, and all four parents come in.

"How did it go?" Ford asks.

Annabelle must hear his voice because she wakes right up and runs over to her parents. Warner pretends he's not checking the baby for damage as he keeps looking him over as he sleeps.

"He's fine, Langley," Kane says.

"Um... we had a situation with Annabelle dragging Jalen in the bouncer to the bathroom, saying he wanted quiet."

Lena looks at Ford, and he cracks up.

"She does that sometimes. Someone's a little jealous." He kisses his daughter's cheek.

"Well, it gave us a heart attack," Kane says. "You should've seen Jana."

"Sorry," Lena says. "At least she didn't draw on him like last time."

I look at Imogen, and she nods with a half smile while Warner inhales a deep breath through flared nostrils.

"Cousins, I guess?" I shrug.

After they thank us, we get into Kane's truck.

"Thank God that's over. Please don't volunteer us again." He pulls out of their driveway.

"I didn't think it was that bad," I say, still trying to figure out what it was I felt seeing Kane with them.

"Not bad? We almost lost one." He laughs, already finding the humor in the situation, then squeezes my knee.

"True." I look out the passenger side window as the houses filled with families pass by.

Why do I suddenly feel as though I'm missing out on something?

CHAPTER 27

Kane

I'm in my office, mentally preparing for the biggest game of my career as a coach so far. If we win this one, then the next one might be the biggest in my coaching career. Year one as a coach and we've already won our division and now we're two wins away from winning the Cup. It's unreal. We've had a grueling six weeks of playoffs, but the guys have given it their all and it's paid off.

There's a knock on the door and I hope like hell it's Jana, because I need some help calming these nerves.

"Come in," I say.

Jana peeks her head in, and relief coats my body. But then her dad is right behind her.

"Oh hi." I should sound more enthusiastic to see the man who put me in this once-in-a-lifetime position.

"Kane, how exciting is this! You know we're a shoo-in," Mr. Gerhardt says.

"It's not over until it's over."

Mr. Gerhardt waves off my concern. "You just keep doing what you've been doing, and it will be fine."

Jana sits back, leaning against the wall with her hands behind her back. She's unreadable, but I'm sure she's as nervous as me. Then again, the closer we get to the Cup, the quieter she's been, as if maybe the pressure is getting to her.

"You've got to give them one helluva speech before they go out on the ice though," Mr. Gerhardt continues.

I really wish he'd leave and give me five minutes alone with his daughter. I don't even want to have sex or make out or cop a feel; I just want her to hold me. Climb into my lap and wrap her arms around me, whispering that we've got this. Although I'd never admit that to anyone.

"I've got it." I hold up the piece of paper I've been jotting notes on. I'm not a veteran coach. I don't have years of practice giving inspirational speeches, but I do have years of sitting on that bench as a player and knowing what got me excited and what didn't.

"Great. Great. Okay, well, I'm going up to the suite. Jana, I'll see you up there?"

"Yep." She nods.

Mr. Gerhardt goes to leave my office, but turns around. I inwardly groan. We're on the clock here.

"I just want to say, I knew you could do it. And I'm proud of you," he says, looking at Jana but then turning in my direction. "Both of you."

He locks eyes with me, and damn, it feels better than anticipated to hear someone say that. Especially the man who put me here. Maybe it's because I never got to hear that from my own parents.

"Thank you. I appreciate you giving me the opportunity."

He nods and walks out the door. I hear the boys already razzing each other to get going and win this thing.

"Come here," I say to Jana.

She pushes off the wall, and I sit back down in my office chair. She sits on my lap just like I wanted and wraps her arms around my neck.

She places a quick kiss on my lips. "No matter what

happens tonight, we got this far. I'm not saying I don't want that Cup, I do, but there was a time during the season when I thought we'd never be here. But you are by far and wide the best coach in this league, and you need to go out there with the confidence and arrogance that drew me to you in the first place."

"My arrogance?"

"Come on. You're Kane Burrows. I might've been slightly intimidated at first."

I chuckle and tighten my arms around her, the smell of her perfume lingering around us and taking my thoughts in the direction of what I want to do with her after this game. "And you were all lady boss, wanting me only for sex."

We laugh, and she kisses my scruffy jaw. "You've got this. I believe in you."

I take her belief and instill it inside me.

The pounding on the door says it's time to give this speech and get out on that ice.

"I gotta go." I give her another quick kiss.

Her hands come up to my cheeks. "Go out there and kick some ass."

"Okay."

"Tell me you will?"

"I will."

"Otherwise, no blow jobs for a year," she says.

"A year, huh? That's quite a commitment for a girl who didn't even want to go on a date after we hooked up."

Her joking smile fades slightly, but she recovers. "I was going to say I was kidding, but maybe now I should say I'm serious."

She smacks a kiss on me before pushing me back. I slide my hand to the back of her head, bringing her lips to mine and giving her a kiss to hold her over until after we win.

"Now you go." She climbs off my lap and offers me her hand, then pulls me up from the chair.

We walk out of my office to where the guys are all dressed and huddled in a circle, waiting.

"Let's go, boys! You've got this!" Jana raises her fist. "Go Fury!"

"Go Fury!" they all shout.

She winks at me and leaves the locker room.

"All right, guys, you know I'm not exactly Shakespeare with my words, so I want a little slack."

I wait for the light chuckling to die down before I start.

"We've been favored to win a lot of this season. We had some ups and downs, but we've persevered every time and come out stronger. This is our moment, boys, time for us to shine as a team. The one thing I love about us is that every player in this room checks his ego at the door because none of you can go out there and win alone. You need everyone else in this room. For some of you, this is your first time being so close to the Cup. Some of you have been here before and lost out. Some of you will never be in this position again. But take all those feelings and throw them away because all that matters is right now and what you do during those three periods out on the ice. The time is now. This game is yours to dominate, to score, to win! So let's go, boys, get out there and kick some ass!"

They all bang their sticks on the floor, shouting, and each of them leaves the locker room with a fist bump from me. I follow with my throat in my stomach, hoping like hell I help them all achieve their dream.

THE FIRST THING I do when I get behind the bench is look up at the suite. Jana is up there with the majority of the wives. Because it's such a big game, they all wanted to be together and have a little privacy, rather than sit in the usual wives and girlfriends' section. In Jana's arms is Jalen with his little headphones over his ears. Imogen blows Warner a kiss, but my gaze goes back to Jana rocking Jalen, not even paying attention to the fact that we've come out.

Ever since we babysat for them... I don't know... she's been quiet about her perimenopause diagnosis. I've noticed her making comments about how cute the kids are in the movies we watch, or when we go on walks on the beach, if there's a family, she's always smiling and telling me how adorable they are. I fear something is changing with her, but she's yet to tell me anything, so I've tried to push away my fears until I know I have something to actually worry about.

The lights go down, and I push Jana and kids and what our future holds to the back of my mind for right now.

The announcers introduce our starters, and they take their turns skating on the ice. From there, it's all a blur.

Warner scores immediately on a play with Aiden and Ford, who circles around the back of the net, shooting it to Warner on the other side, who flips it into the top corner of the net. The three of them are phenomenal together and have definitely found their groove the last half of this season.

Maksim helps Matt McIntosh in the net soon after, blocking Los Angeles from scoring, and gets the puck back to Ford, who skates up the left side but gets hammered into the wall. Ford gets up and pushes the other player, and they both end up in the sin bin.

Los Angeles gets by us in the second and scores a goal, tying the game.

It's back and forth, but when Tweetie, Cory, and Train get in with a minute to go in the second period, they do the same play the first line did to score the first goal except this time Cory's the one who scores. The crowd goes crazy. LA tries to get a point before the period ends, but they're unsuccessful.

Between the second and third periods, Imogen's assistant keeps the crowd entertained. Imogen's more a hype planner now, while someone else sees it through.

In the locker room, we go over some plays and over their defense and what we've seen so far this game. When we return to the ice, my gaze goes to the suite again. This time, Jana waves to me, but quickly gets distracted by something at her side. She scoops up Annabelle and they both wave to me. I've never seen her with the kids this much, but maybe I'm seeing things because of how upset she was after the doctor's news.

The third period starts and LA scores within the first thirty seconds.

Fuck. Not a good way to start the last period.

A few minutes later, we make a comeback. Warner skates all the way down the ice, rushing past their defense and passing to Aiden at the last minute. He scores from an ungodly angle only Aiden would be capable of. Which makes us up by a goal. The Fury fans are going nuts, but one goal is way too close to assume we're going to win.

Maksim and our defensemen do an excellent job at keeping Los Angeles at bay, but at the end of the third period, LA gets a breakaway. I hold my breath, watching Matt in the net. Being a goalie myself, I know the amount of pressure there is on him in this scenario. You don't have any backup. It's just you and the guy with the puck and you have to read where he's going with it.

"Oh shit," Cory says next to me.

LA's center brings his stick back, and it's like it all happens in slow motion. One of those nail-biters that ESPN will analyze over and over about how it might have gone.

It's going to the bottom right, I can see it, and I can only hope that with all the work I've done with Matt since the start of the season, he sees it too.

Sure enough, the center shoots the puck, and everyone watches as the puck flies toward the goal. I could kiss Matt, because he falls to his knees, blocking the puck with his left shin guard. The puck flies off in the other direction as the third-period buzzer sounds and our bench clears, everyone skating over to Matt to congratulate him.

I remain behind the bench, watching it all unfold, and study the look on Matt's face. For the first time, I really fall in love with coaching. A rookie who just got drafted has made the game-defining play. It just doesn't get better than that.

We all head to the locker room after, and Jana gets off the elevator just as I'm about to make my way inside. She runs to me, and I pick her up and swing her around.

"I knew you could do it," she says. "And Matt, seriously? What a play!"

"You always have a thing for goalies?" I lower her to the floor.

"I only have a thing for one goalie who is now the best coach in the league."

"We still have one more game," I tell her, then kiss her.

"And you'll win that one too."

We do the press conference, and while everyone else goes to celebrate, I take my girl home because she's the only person I want to celebrate with.

CHAPTER 28

"So where do we go from here?"
—Jana

Jana

I walk into Kane's bedroom with the tray of breakfast items I made. Not to be too full of myself, but I think I did a pretty great job. The eggs look fluffy, the toast is lightly browned, the fruit's been cut up and placed in a bowl.

After we returned from the game last night, we made love. Kane's movements were slow and loving, and the words he said were sweet and endearing. I wonder if we lost, if I would've had a different Kane in bed with me.

But I feel us moving into a new stage of our relationship. Neither of us ever wants to be away from the other. He's my first call out of work, and it's usually to decide about dinner. We spend all our time together, and though it's not official, I've practically moved in with him I'm at his place so much. I'm not even scared to admit that I love him anymore. I mean, he's the best man I've ever known.

There's just one problem that I've yet to bring up to him. Since my diagnosis and babysitting Jalen and Annabelle, I can't get rid of this feeling in my gut that maybe I've been wrong all these years. Maybe I really do want to be a mother. It didn't help that I went with Paisley to her doctor's appointment when Maksim was out of town and could only be on FaceTime. When they heard the heartbeat, the way they looked at each other... I think I want that with Kane. But I'm waiting until after the Cup to broach this subject.

He was good with the kids when we babysat, even if he said he didn't want to be there. Maybe he'd change his mind? I don't think either of us ever thought our relationship would turn into love. It's just a simple change of circumstance, right?

Rocky's ears perk up when he smells that I have food.

"You get enough scraps," I whisper and place the tray on the side table. "Kane baby." I kiss his cheek and my hand runs up his back. "Breakfast for the number one coach."

He stirs in the bed, then grabs me, pulling me into bed with him.

"Ugh, you!" I playfully smack him. "You were up the whole time."

He gets me on my back and kisses my cheek. "You in the kitchen isn't exactly as quiet as a library," he says, kissing my other cheek.

"Remind me never to do anything nice for you again."

He slides between my legs and his hard length grinds against my core, making me forget about the eggs getting cold.

"I only want one thing for breakfast and that's you." He kisses my neck and down to my collarbone.

Just like last night, he explores my body from my neck down to between my legs in a slow, meticulous manner. When he finally pushes inside me, that feeling I know to be love nestles deep within me.

He pushes in and out, circling his hips, saying words of praise about my body and how the two of us together are magic. I grip his shoulder blades, not wanting an inch between us, not wanting the warmth of him to go away, never wanting this intimacy to end.

"Kane, I... oh god." I clench hard and try not to come.

He sees the signs, as he always does, and picks up his pace slightly. His hand travels down my side and between my legs, where his finger deftly circles my clit. All the sensation concentrates in my core, and I explode into a million glittering pieces, my back surging off the bed, and the words I've tried so hard to keep inside while we make love slip from my mouth.

"I love you," I whisper. "I want to be with you forever."

Kane stops midthrust. My eyes pop open and he's staring at me. "What did you just say?"

I adamantly shake my head. "Nothing. Just keep going." I move my hands to his ass, pushing him inside me. "Forget it."

"Did you just say you want to be with me forever?" He doesn't pay any attention to me trying to continue the sex. "Did you say it because of the orgasm?"

Okay, Jana, just be honest. That's all you can do. Don't play games. Be an adult about this. I bite my lip and shake my head.

"You meant it?"

I nod.

"Say it again, baby."

"Kane."

"Say it." He kisses me once.

"I love you and want to be with you forever."

A slow grin with a devilish glint forms on his lips. "I feel the same."

Then he's thrusting hard inside me, kissing me and holding me closer. He stills inside me, pumping a few times and emptying himself before rolling over to his side.

He helps me get cleaned up, and after I go to the bathroom, I crawl into bed where he already has the tray of food out. So far, he hasn't mentioned our declarations again, and it makes me nervous. I know there's something we have to discuss before I can feel settled in the knowledge that we want to be together forever.

And it's not marriage. I don't care about an engagement or a wedding or anything like that. I could remain with Kane in the same way we exist now for eternity.

"Oh, these eggs are good," he mumbles over a mouthful.

"I'm glad you like them." I pick up a strawberry and eat it.

Rocky whines at the side of the bed.

Kane eats his entire meal and says nothing about what just happened, and now I'm more nervous than ever to discuss what we need to. I move to turn on the television to see what the analysts are saying about last night's game, but he takes the remote from my hand.

"Later." He pulls me to his chest. "Let's talk more about how you want to spend forever with me."

"Oh my god!" I slap his chest and try to get up, but he holds me there. "You wait for the whole breakfast to talk about it."

"I might have to hold it over your head forever that you said it first."

"Fine. I'm just an honest person."

He runs his hand down my arm, goose bumps following their path. "Last night..."

"Was amazing," I say, turning to look up at him. Didn't he think last night was amazing?

"It was, but I noticed you seem more comfortable with Jalen and Annabelle now, eh?"

This is it. I told myself that I would bring this up after the Cup. There's no reason to cause a rift in our relationship before such an important game. But if I don't say anything now, it'll feel like I'm lying.

"Yeah. I guess when you almost lose one..." I chuckle.

He doesn't.

Another stretch of silence hangs between us.

"Jana?" It's clear from his tone what he's asking, so I sit up from his chest to face him.

I cross my legs and he stays lying down on the bed, his fingers running along my legs.

"You seem to enjoy it. And after the doctor's appointment, I'm just wondering if..."

"I've changed my mind?" I finish the sentence for him in a whisper.

He nods.

I cringe. "Maybe? I think so. I don't know."

He waits patiently for me to continue.

Emotion overwhelms me, because as much as I've been trying to ignore what I feel about having a child, it's impossible. But I know there's also a very real possibility that this new realization could cost me my relationship with Kane.

A tear slips down my cheek as I nod. "I think I do want a child."

He sits up, wrapping his arms around me and letting me cry all over his chest. He's so stoic that I can't tell what he's thinking.

"I never thought I wanted to have kids... but I don't know if it's the fact that the doctor told me I can't if I wait too much longer or if it's because when we babysat, I saw you with Annabelle and Jalen and I pictured us with our own kids... maybe it's just that now that I'm in a relationship with a man I love and trust and want to spend the rest of my life with, it feels natural to want children with him. Whatever the reason, my feelings have changed."

He continues to run his hand up and down my back, but doesn't say anything.

"You'd be a great dad," I whisper, hoping it will urge him to respond.

His hand freezes on my back. "I'm never going to be a dad, Jana."

His confession is like a knife piercing my heart, because I hear the resolve in his voice.

I draw back and look at him. "What?"

Sitting up, he brings his knees up and rests his arms on his knees, clasping his hands together in between. "I understand you changing your mind, but I haven't changed mine. I don't want kids."

More tears fall down my cheeks and I wipe them away. "So where do we go from here?"

Pain flashes across his face and he shrugs. "I'm never going to change my mind. I don't want to be a parent."

My chest squeezes painfully, making it hard to breathe. "But—"

"We can keep going around with this, but nothing's going to change. We want different things now, and honestly"—he looks me directly in the eye—"I love you too much to not make sure you get everything you want out of life."

Somehow, that hurts more.

"But I want you." I crawl toward him.

"Believe me, I want you too. More than anything." He stares into my eyes and cups the side of my face. I lean into his warmth. "I went from the highest of highs when you said you wanted to be with me forever to the lowest of lows because I can't give the woman I love what she wants. Not without resentment on my part."

The word resentment is the needle that pops the balloon. I would never want him to resent me for pressuring him to do something he doesn't really want.

I can't do this. I can't be here anymore.

I climb out of bed, grab my clothes from yesterday, and get dressed.

"Jana, you don't have to run off," Kane says from the bed.

I ignore him and rush out to the living area. The doorbell rings, but I grab my purse from the kitchen counter.

"Just wait, Jana." Kane follows me toward the front door.

"It's fine. I completely understand. I just need to be alone." I open up the front door and Lee stands there.

"Oh shit, I knew it was early, but—"

"Hi, Lee. You came for the Cup. What a great brother you are. You two have fun."

"Jana?" Lee asks, then looks into the house. "Seriously, bro. Put some damn pants on."

I get in my car and peel out of his driveway. My tires squeal as I race far away as fast as I can. And somehow end up outside Paisley's house.

Maksim opens the door, but I walk right past him and into Paisley's waiting arms.

CHAPTER 29

Kane

"What the hell just happened?" Lee walks into my house. "You two should've been on cloud nine. You could win the Cup tomorrow!"

I shake my head and go down the hall to my bedroom, ignoring the crushing pain in my chest. "Take Rocky out while I get dressed."

Lee turns his attention to Rocky. "Come on, Rock, I wish you could tell me how your master fucked up. Grab your ball."

I stop at the doorway to my bedroom. Taking in how it all went to shit. Why did I have to ask? Maybe I should have left it alone. I could've let us live in our love bubble and ignored that my gut was telling me something had changed.

Shaking my head, I go to my dresser and pull on some shorts and a T-shirt. I hear Lee talking to someone on the other end of the deck before I open the French doors in my bedroom to join him.

"I'm Kane's brother, Lee. I play for the San Francisco Kingsmen. Quarterback."

If anything could make me laugh right now, it's Lee flirting with Emma, so I remain out of sight for a second.

"Oh really? He never told me about you." Emma's playing along, because she knows about Lee. He hasn't been here a lot in the past two years that I've lived here, but I've told her and Sam about my brother.

"Yeah, I'm his younger brother. We didn't make it to the playoffs this year, but we've got a promising year coming up. We had the first draft pick, so we got a killer wide receiver."

"Doesn't that mean you were the worst team in the league?" Emma asks, and I bite my fist to not laugh out loud.

"Well, it's a developmental year."

I decide to save my little brother and his bad flirting. "Hey, you two."

"I was just coming over to check why I saw Jana tearing out of the driveway?" Emma leaves my brother's side while he keeps throwing the ball for Rocky.

"Nothing. It was just a... nothing."

She props a hand on her hip. "Bullshit. What did you do? That ego getting too big?"

Before I can answer, our attention is drawn to the sound of vehicles on our quiet street. I catch a glimpse of a few of them and know who they belong to.

"Why does everyone think they can be in my business?"

Emma shrugs. "I don't think your brother realizes I'm a lesbian," she whispers.

"You think?"

"Is that your dog Rocky's humping?" Lee asks Emma.

Sure enough, Rocky and Penny are going at it on the beach.

"Ugh, your damn dog!"

While Emma runs off to stop the dogs, a line of hockey players comes through my side gate.

I raise my hand before they can say anything. "Nope. I don't need any of you to give me some 'come to your senses' speech. We were on the same page. She changed her mind and that's fair. She's allowed to do so. I still love her, but it's over."

My brother whips in my direction, dropping Rocky's ball on the deck. "What do you mean, she changed her mind?"

"He doesn't want kids and Jana does," Cory says.

Jesus, these guys are worse than a bunch of old biddies gossiping around a sewing circle.

Lee's jaw drops open. "What do you mean you don't want kids? I thought you wanted a family."

"Why would I want a family?" I shout before lowering my voice. "I've already helped raise you. Mom fell apart the day Dad died and the onus was on me." I walk off the deck and head down to the beach, wanting everyone to leave me alone with this feeling of emptiness at knowing Jana and I can't work.

But no such luck, because my brother follows me. "So what? You'll be there to raise your kid."

I whip around to face him. "But what if I'm not? I'm sure Dad didn't think he was gonna die. And I'm sure he didn't think Mom would crumble into a depression and never crawl her way out."

"And what? You think Jana's gonna wallow forever if you die?"

Some of the guys on the deck chuckle, obviously still able to hear us.

"I kind of hope so," I say.

"Sure, she'd mourn you, but a woman like Jana isn't gonna do what Mom did to us. She's gonna pick herself up and raise your children. Think back to the way Mom was before Dad died. I was young, but hell, even I can remember."

"We're just gonna go inside," Warner says, and they all head inside my house.

"What are you talking about?"

"She was always more about him than us. She always made what he wanted for dinner, always told us not to disturb him for at least a half hour when he came home from work. On the weekends, we weren't supposed to wake him up if he slept late or if he was napping on the couch in the living room. And when it came to hockey or football, Dad was in charge of taking us. He came to our games and practices and cheered us on. Mom didn't want any part of it. Even before Dad died, Mom was never that involved in our lives. Honestly, I think she always had a predisposition to be how she is, and Dad's death just put her over the edge."

It's been a long time since I thought of who my mom was before my dad's accident. I guess I forgot. But Lee's right. She was exactly the way he's describing her.

"Listen, I know I don't know Jana the way you do, but she doesn't seem like the type who folds under a challenge. She seems like the kind of woman who looks at a challenge head-on and pushes through—as painful and difficult as it might be. Jana would raise your kids with or without you and make sure they succeed in life."

I sit down in the sand. "But what if that's not what would happen? How could I take that chance? This is a child we're talking about."

Lee plops down next to me. "I always knew you had a big head, but I never thought you were this arrogant. Think you're so fucking awesome, Jana won't ever find someone after you? Or even if she doesn't, that she won't love her children enough to pull herself together and raise them?"

"Mom didn't."

"I know," he says softly. "But she does love us. She told me to tell you good luck."

"She watched the game?"

He shakes his head. "No, I told her about it."

I nod, upset with myself for expecting more.

"Honestly, Kane, do you love her?"

"Yeah. With everything that I am."

"And the only reason you don't want kids is because of how we grew up? You're scared?"

It takes me a moment to admit it, but I nod. Terrified would be a more apt descriptor.

"Then give your child the one thing you didn't have. Give them a childhood. Watch it through their eyes. Can you really not see yourself and Jana having a child?"

I shrug. "It's hard to let go of twenty years of resentment toward Mom and telling myself I would never be a dad. But yeah, there was a moment when we were watching our friends' kids... she had Warner's son, Jalen, and yeah, I wondered what if, but..."

"Then why are you still here?"

I look at him. "What do you mean?"

"Right now, you're losing the only woman you've ever loved because you're scared. The big brother I know doesn't let anything scare him. Or if it did, he pushed through and confronted it straight on. You never used to let fear dictate what you wanted for yourself. What happened?"

He's right. I push a hand through my hair. "Jesus, I'm a dick."

"I've been telling you that for years."

I ignore his jab and jog into the house, where I find the guys eating every snack I have in the cabinets and the fridge.

"Where is she?" I ask, looking at each one in turn.

Maksim's head pops out of my fridge. "Come with me."

CHAPTER 30

Jana

"I can't even fault him," I say to Paisley. "We were in agreement before we ever fell in love."

I hold her pillow to my chest. Maksim left an hour ago, and I have a pretty good guess where he went.

Paisley's phone dings. "You changed your mind. You're allowed to. Sounds like he's being stubborn."

"No, he's not." I can't fault him. I'm the one who changed my mind about what I wanted.

"You probably want to change your clothes, right? You're still in last night's outfit," Paisley says.

"No, it's okay. I'll go home in a little bit."

"You should go now." Paisley stands with much effort now that her belly has really popped and takes the pillow off my lap. "What if someone surprises you with an interview after last night's win and you're wearing what you wore last night? Not a good look." She leads me by the elbow toward the front door. "You go and I'll meet you there in a bit."

"What? But..." I pick up my purse and dig for my keys. "Do you have somewhere you have to be or something?"

She shakes her head. "No, I'll be right over. But you should go shower and stuff, then we'll continue this conversation."

"God, Paisley, you're kicking me out now?"

"I'm protecting you." She opens the door and practically shoos me out, leaving me outside their front door. "I'll be right behind you, just let me lock up. I'll grab Starbucks."

I stand there for a second. Maybe she's sick of my "woe is me" act she's endured for the past hour. Especially since nothing will change about our situation.

Still feeling bereft, I get in my car and drive to my house, but I stop at Starbucks first because she probably won't get my order correct.

At home, I park and climb out of my car, heading to the front door, but I take a step back when I spot someone sitting there. "Whoa!"

When he looks up, it takes me a second to register that it's Kane. He stands and runs his hand down his beard. His lips are downturned, and his eyes appear unsure. "Hey."

"Hi." Going around him, I use my keys to unlock the door. I turn around before he can follow me inside. "You didn't have to come. I understand. I really do. We'll be friends... eventually. I just need some time to get over us. I promise, no hard feelings." Just complete and utter heartbreak, but I'm not telling him that.

"Maksim dropped me off."

"Oh." That explains Paisley's act.

"I figured we should plan." He comes into the house, one cautious step at a time.

"Plan what?" I set my purse on the foyer table, along with my keys.

"Well, I figure if we're going to do this, we need to really do it right. I've never half assed anything in my life. So, we should get married before we have kids, and we should probably move in here or add an addition to my place. But you have more room here." He gestures absently to our surroundings.

"Kane..." I sigh, my shoulders falling. I love him for what he's trying to do, but no.

"How many bedrooms do you have? I only have the extra one, so if we only have one kid, we'll be okay, but you saw Warner and how much stuff Jalen had."

I continue into the house and sit on my couch while he sits on the chair adjacent to me. "Please stop. I won't ever let you resent me. You don't have to do this."

He falls to his knees in front of me. "That's the thing. I'll hate myself if I let you slip out of my fingers. My brother helped me realize that fear has been holding me back. I never stopped to question my own assumptions. You're not my mom. Some people say a son falls for a replica of his mom, but I fell in love with a woman who is the complete opposite. You're strong and independent and comfortable in your skin. Everything I love about you is the reason you're going to be a rock star of a mom."

"Kane, I don't want—"

He places his finger on my lips. "I'm not doing this just because this is what you want. I'm not gonna lie, when we babysat and I saw you with Jalen, I did think what if... the whole night, except for losing Jalen, I felt like we were playing house and I thought maybe we could do this, we'd be good at it. But I pushed that thought away because of fear. Fear that what happened to me could happen to my own child in some form or another. I don't want to live my life in fear. Not when it comes to you, the most fearless woman I've ever known."

"What are you saying?" I ask, wanting to hear the words come out of his mouth.

"First, I'm asking you to marry me."

"Kane!" I bring my legs up and cross them, shaking my head.

"I don't have a ring, but marry me, Jana. And throw away your pills. Let's just jump into this headfirst. We wasted a year screwing around, then we wasted months pretending to hate each other. I don't want to waste any more time."

He grips my hips and pulls me to the end of the sofa. I wasn't lying when I said I didn't need to be married to be content with Kane forever, but something about this feels right.

"Okay," I whisper and nod, tears building in my eyes.

"How about some enthusiasm there?"

"Okay," I say a little louder.

"Okay what?"

"Yes! I'll marry you and throw away my pills on one condition."

He tilts his head. "What's that?"

"We move into your house. Maybe down the road we can add on or move, but I want us to live where we fell in love and that's where I fell in love with you. In that small two-bedroom house on the beach."

He grins and nods. "Done."

He presses his lips to mine, sealing our agreement with a kiss.

EPILOGUE

"Congratulations to the happy couple!"

Kane

Florida Fury won the Stanley Cup.

The headlines were on every paper in the country, and the articles detailed the 2–0 shutout. Every player had a part in the win, and to see my players come together as a team was the most rewarding part for me as a coach.

Each player took the Cup for their designated time and spent it in different ways.

Aiden took it to his family in Wisconsin, showed it off at his parents' bar, and the triplets decided they're going to win one of their own one day. He and Saige are planning a big wedding up in Wisconsin before next season starts.

Maksim hung out at home and FaceTimed his family in Russia. Immediately after we won the Cup, Paisley gave birth to a healthy baby girl they named Kira, and she and Maksim are settling into parenthood well.

Ford mostly sat Annabelle in it and took a lot of pictures. He and Lena are considering having another child sooner rather than later, to help Annabelle adjust to not being the only child in the family.

Warner took the Cup to New York and showed it off to his mom and his brother and sister. He gave an inspirational speech for underprivileged youth who use the services his charitable foundation provides and they each got to touch it. And Jalen was baptized in the Cup. Not sure how they pulled off that one.

Cory and Ande took it to an inner-city youth camp, where Cory showed off some of his skills and showed them what hard work can accomplish. He also proposed to Ande with the ring in the Cup. I guess he gets points for being original.

As for me, I decided the Cup would be with me on the beach while I eloped with the love of my life. No one else was invited. So the Stanley Cup sits at a table not far from where Jana walks toward me in a simple white gown. I'm wearing a khaki suit, nothing fancy.

She looks absolutely radiant, and the emerald-and-diamond ring I bought her sparkles in the island sun. Her long blonde hair blows in the gentle breeze, and I swear I hold my breath the entire time she makes her way toward me.

We didn't want to wait to get married since the kid thing is a big unknown. Will Jana have to do IVF, will she get pregnant the natural way, will we need to involve a surrogate? These are all questions we have to find the answers to, but we decided to wait until after our wedding before we started searching for them. We wanted today to be about our love, our commitment, and the possibility of what might be going forward.

Jana reaches me and takes my hand.

"You look stunning." I can't take my eyes off her.

She smiles and gives me the once-over. "You clean up pretty well yourself."

She winks because she's seen me much more dressed up than this, but I did trim down my beard and get my hair trimmed for the occasion. Can't have the wifey thinking I've let myself go just because I'm about to become married to her.

The officiant we met only an hour ago begins the ceremony. And when he tells me it's my turn to say my vows, I speak from the heart.

"Jana, as we stand here today, I want to thank you for showing me what real love is. Despite your stubborn, high-maintenance side, I knew there was something special about you."

She rolls her eyes playfully.

"You're a strong, powerful, fearless woman who doesn't make apologies for who you are, and I admire that, as much as that side of you drives me crazy sometimes." I squeeze her hands and wink. "I cannot imagine my life without you. Your presence has allowed me to imagine a life I never thought would be possible for me. Knowing you're by my side allows me to step away from my fear and embrace all the possibilities of what might be, because with you by my side, I know that whatever happens, it will turn out all right. I love you more than I can put into words, and I need you to know that you are everything to me. Without you, my life has no meaning. It just doesn't make sense."

By the time I finish, she has tears in her eyes.

The officiant directs Jana to say her vows, and like me, she doesn't have anything written down.

"Kane, I never could have anticipated how much my life would change when you walked into it. In all honesty, looking back, I don't even feel like I was really living before you became a part of my life. I was just sort of existing. You've loved me in a way that few ever have before—unconditionally. And there is such peace in knowing that no matter what, you will be there cheering me on, picking up the pieces of me if I fall apart, and loving me in a way I never knew was possible. I love you with all that I am, all that I have, and all that I can be. And no matter what the future holds for us, we will deal with it together. And that's all I need to know that this union today will have a happy ending."

I sniff back my own tears and have to use the cuff of my suit jacket to wipe my face.

Eventually the officiant pronounces us husband and wife, and I pull Jana into my arms and kiss her with the love and tenderness that flows through my veins. The lady boss is officially my wife. Who would have thought?

We take some pictures for social media with us and the Cup, then we send it home with the two trustees, since we were the last ones from the team to get it.

My career has been a long one, relatively speaking, and I feared that the best part of my life was over when I retired and went into coaching. Now, with this silver ring on my left finger, I feel as though the best is still to come. Like I have a whole new life to start with this amazing woman by my side.

IT'S early morning when my phone rings, and I see that it's my brother. I put him on speaker because I'm too lazy to hold the phone to my ear. Jana and I have been sex fiends since the wedding yesterday, and I'm still recuperating.

"Hey, Lee," I say. "You're on speaker."

"Congratulations to the happy couple! Aren't you glad I got his head out of his ass for you, sis?"

Something warms in my chest at hearing my brother refer to my new wife as sis.

She giggles next to me, naked in our honeymoon bed. "Thank you for the millionth time."

"You're interrupting sex time," I say.

"Sorry, I just wanted to call and give my congrats, but I had to tell you... you're never gonna believe who I just found out has been hired as my team's massage therapist?"

I forgot training camp has already started for him. "Who?"

"Shayna Kudrow."

My eyes bug out of my head, and Jana looks at me in confusion.

"Didn't you..." I start, and Jana frowns.

"I did."

"This should be interesting." I scratch my beard.

"Real interesting. Anyway, gotta go, but I knew you'd be the only one who would understand how fucked up this is."

We hang up.

Jana sits up, turning to face me. "What did he do?"

"You're my wife, so no secrets, right?"

She gives me a stern nod in only the way she can. "That's right."

So I tell her the history of Lee Burrows and Shayna Kudrow...

The End

Cockamamie Unicorn Ramblings

As we've always said in our ramblings, some couples take longer than others to connect with when you're writing a book. Sometimes it's not until the end of the book when an author finally knows their character. But with Jana and Kane, something sparked by the second chapter.

We've teased you from the start of Tropical Hat Trick about these two. Many times we write those little pieces without fleshing out their characters or their story and we end up in the corner somewhere wondering how the heck we can write ourselves out of it.

And that kind of happened here. Kane was originally going to want kids and a family from the get-go. He'd want the relationship and fight for Jana. But there were some reasons why this didn't work for us so one long Zoom call later we decided to switch up the storyline a little, bringing you what you just read.

We know a few people weren't fond of Jana in some of the previous books and we're hoping she won you over in the end. One of our goals is to give you different types of characters throughout a series. We don't want them to ever be carbon copies of each other. We aspire for you to know their personalities and what makes each one a little different than another. Within a series and sometimes when they're only a secondary character in someone else's book you can't see their actual story yet and you might not under-stand them. You might not get why they do what they do.

But know that we always (usually) have a plan. LOL Jana was definitely the right fit for Kane, and she needed a guy like Kane who was strong enough to stand up to her and strong enough to fight for her.

All in all, this is one of our favorites in the series and we hope it's yours as well!

As always, we have to thank the village that helped get this book into your hands!

The entire Valentine PR Team.
Cassie from Joy Editing for line edits.
Ellie from My Brother's Editor for line edits.
Rosa from My Brother's Editor for proofreading.
Hang Le for the cover and branding for the entire series.
Wander Aguiar for the photo. We're pretty sure this entire series covers can set your bookshelf on fire!
Bloggers who consistently carve out time to read, review and/or promote our work.
Piper Rayne Unicorns who are so much fun to chat with! Thank you for loving these little worlds we create!
Every reader who took the time to read our story—whether it's your first Piper Rayne book or your fiftieth. We hope we provided you with a few hours of entertainment.
It's sad to say goodbye to the Hockey Hotties, but exciting news, we're heading over to the other side of the U.S. for Lee Burrows' (Kane's brother) story, where he's kicking off our new series, Kingsmen Football Stars. We're sure there will be some cameos of our much loved hockey stars so you're not saying goodbye forever.

xo,
Piper & Rayne

ABOUT PIPER & RAYNE

Piper Rayne is a USA Today Bestselling Author duo who write "heartwarming humor with a side of sizzle" about families, whether that be blood or found. They both have e-readers full of one-clickable books, they're married to husbands who drive them to drink, and they're both chauffeurs to their kids. Most of all, they love hot heroes and quirky heroines who make them laugh, and they hope you do, too!

ALSO BY PIPER RAYNE

Hockey Hotties

My Lucky #13

The Trouble with #9

Faking it with #41

Sneaking around with #34

Second Shot with #76

Offside with #55

Kingsmen Football Stars

You had your chance, Lee Burrows

You can't kiss the Nanny, Brady Banks

Over my Brother's Dead Body, Chase Andrews

The Baileys

Lessons from a One-Night Stand

Advice from a Jilted Bride

Birth of a Baby Daddy

Operation Bailey Wedding (Novella)

Falling for My Brother's Best Friend

Demise of a Self-Centered Playboy

Confessions of a Naughty Nanny

Operation Bailey Babies (Novella)

Secrets of the World's Worst Matchmaker

Winning My Best Friend's Girl

Rules for Dating your Ex

Operation Bailey Birthday (Novella)

The Greenes

My Beautiful Neighbor

My Almost Ex

My Vegas Groom

The Greene Family Summer Bash

My Sister's Flirty Friend

My Unexpected Surprise

My Famous Frenemy

The Greene Family Vacation

My Scorned Best Friend

My Fake Fiancé

My Brother's Forbidden Friend

The Modern Love World

Charmed by the Bartender

Hooked by the Boxer

Mad about the Banker

The Single Dad's Club

Real Deal

Dirty Talker

Sexy Beast

Hollywood Hearts

Mister Mom

Animal Attraction

Domestic Bliss

Bedroom Games
Cold as Ice
On Thin Ice
Break the Ice
Box Set

Charity Case
Manic Monday
Afternoon Delight
Happy Hour

Blue Collar Brothers
Flirting with Fire
Crushing on the Cop
Engaged to the EMT

White Collar Brothers
Sexy Filthy Boss
Dirty Flirty Enemy
Wild Steamy Hook-up

The Rooftop Crew
My Bestie's Ex
A Royal Mistake
The Rival Roomies
Our Star-Crossed Kiss
The Do-Over

A Co-Workers Crush